ABB CHR

Christie, A.
Sparkling cyanide.

PRICE: $20.00 (3798/abbarp)

Agatha Christie

Sparkling Cyanide

ST. THOMAS PUBLIC LIBRARY

D1113430

Collins

AUG - - 2019

Collins

HarperCollins Publishers
The News Building
1 London Bridge Street
London SE1 9GF

www.collinselt.com

Collins® is a registered trademark of HarperCollins Publishers Limited.

This *Collins English Readers* edition first published by HarperCollins Publishers 2017.

10 9 8 7 6 5 4 3 2 1

First published in Great Britain by Collins 1945

Copyright © 1945 Agatha Christie Limited. All rights reserved.
AGATHA CHRISTIE and the Agatha Christie Signature are registered trade marks of Agatha Christie Limited in the UK and elsewhere. All rights reserved.

www.agathachristie.com

ISBN: 978-0-00-826234-1

A catalogue record for this book is available from the British Library.

Cover design © HarperCollins*Publishers* Ltd/Agatha Christie Ltd 2017

Typeset by Davidson Publishing Solutions, Glasgow

Printed and bound by CPI Group (UK) Ltd., Croydon, CR0 4YY

All rights reserved. No part of this publication may be reproduced, stored in a retrieval system, or transmitted, in any form or by any means, electronic, mechanical, photocopying, recording or otherwise, without the prior permission of the publishers.

This book is sold subject to the condition that it shall not, by way of trade or otherwise, be lent, re-sold, hired out or otherwise circulated without the publisher's prior consent in any form of binding or cover other than that in which it is published and without a similar condition including this condition being imposed on the subsequent purchaser.

HarperCollins does not warrant that www.collinselt.com or any other website mentioned in this title will be provided uninterrupted, that any website will be error free, that defects will be corrected, or that the website or the server that makes it available are free of viruses or bugs. For full terms and conditions please refer to the site terms provided on the website.

Contents

✦ Introduction ✦

About Collins English Readers

Collins English Readers have been created for readers worldwide whose first language is not English. The stories are carefully graded to ensure that you, the reader, will both enjoy and benefit from your reading experience.

Words which are above the required reading level are underlined the first time they appear in a story. All underlined words are defined in the **Glossary** at the back of the book. Books at levels 1 and 2 take their definitions from the *Collins COBUILD Essential English Dictionary*, and books at levels 3 and above from the *Collins COBUILD Advanced English Dictionary*. Where appropriate, definitions are simplified for level and context.

Alongside the glossary, a **Character list** is provided to help the reader identify who is who, and how they are connected to each other. **Cultural notes** explain historical, cultural and other references. **Maps and diagrams** are provided where appropriate. A **downloadable recording** is also available of the full story. To access the audio, go to www.collinselt.com/eltreadersaudio. The password is the second word on page 5 of this book.

To support both teachers and learners, additional materials are available online at www.collinselt.com/readers. These include a **Plot synopsis** and **classroom activities** (both for teachers), **Student activities**, a **level checker** and much more.

About Agatha Christie

Agatha Christie (1890–1976) is known throughout the world as the Queen of Crime. She is the most widely published and translated author of all time and in any language; only the Bible and Shakespeare have sold more copies.

Agatha Christie's first novel was published in 1920. It featured Hercule Poirot, the Belgian detective who has become the most popular detective in crime fiction since Sherlock Holmes.

Collins has published Agatha Christie since 1926.

The Grading Scheme

The Collins COBUILD Grading Scheme has been created using the most up-to-date language usage information available today. Each level is guided by a comprehensive grammar and vocabulary framework, ensuring that the series will perfectly match readers' abilities.

		CEF band	Pages	Word count	Headwords
Level 1	elementary	A2	64	5,000–8,000	approx. 700
Level 2	pre-intermediate	A2–B1	80	8,000–11,000	approx. 900
Level 3	intermediate	B1	96	11,000–20,000	approx. 1,300
Level 4	upper-intermediate	B2	112-128	15,000–26,000	approx. 1,700
Level 5	upper-intermediate+	B2+	128+	22,000–30,000	approx. 2,200
Level 6	advanced	C1	144+	28,000+	2,500+
Level 7	advanced+	C2	160+	*varied*	*varied*

For more information on the Collins COBUILD Grading Scheme go to www.collinselt.com/readers/gradingscheme.

Book 1
Rosemary

Rosemary Barton died from cyanide[1] poisoning, nearly a year ago...

.... Chapter 1 ....
Iris Marle

Iris Marle was thinking about her sister, Rosemary Barton. For nearly a year she had tried to forget the blue face, the twisted fingers... The difference between that and the lovely, happy Rosemary of the day before... Well, perhaps not happy. She had been ill – she was tired and depressed. That's why she had killed herself, wasn't it?

But last night Rosemary's husband, George Barton, had called her into his study and shown her those letters. And now she had to remember the past.

Pictures came into her mind. Herself as a small child, eating bread and milk, and Rosemary, six years older, doing school work at a table. Rosemary going to boarding school, and coming home for the holidays. Rosemary going to live in Paris, and coming home an elegant, beautiful woman, with red-gold hair and dark blue eyes.

Rosemary's life became full of late breakfasts in bed, lunches with girlfriends and evening dances – while Iris still went to school, walked in the parks, ate supper at nine o'clock and was in bed by ten.

And then, Rosemary had married George Barton. Iris still wondered why. So many exciting young men had been taking her out, while George Barton was fifteen years older than herself, kind, pleasant, and extremely dull. It wasn't money. Rosemary already had Uncle Paul's money. Paul Bennett wasn't really an uncle. He had been in love with their mother, but she had chosen another, poorer man, Hector Marle. Paul had accepted his defeat and remained a family friend. He had become known as Uncle Paul, and was <u>godfather</u> to Rosemary. When he died, he left his entire fortune to his thirteen-year-old <u>goddaughter</u>[2]. So why had the rich and beautiful Rosemary married boring George Barton? She hadn't loved him. But she had been happy with him and was very fond of him.

A year later, Iris and Rosemary's mother, Viola Marle, had died. Their father, Hector, had died many years before, and so, at the age of seventeen, Iris went to live with Rosemary and George in Elvaston Square.

◆ ◆ ◆

Iris had not seen much of her sister in those days. Rosemary was always out shopping, or going to parties. But she had seemed happy enough until that day, a week before it happened, when Iris had entered Rosemary's sitting room to find her sitting at her desk and <u>weeping</u> <u>bitterly</u>. Iris had never seen Rosemary cry before. It frightened her, although Rosemary had been ill with <u>influenza</u> and she knew that it could leave you depressed.

'Rosemary, what's wrong?' she cried.

Rosemary wiped her <u>tear-stained</u> face. 'Nothing!' she said, angrily. Then she stood up and ran out of the room. Puzzled, Iris walked over to the table, and saw her own name on a piece of paper. Rosemary had been writing to her! She read the note.

Darling Iris,

There isn't any point in making a <u>will</u>[2] because my money goes to you anyway, but I'd like some of my things to be given to particular people.

> *To George, the jewellery he's given me.*
> *To Gloria King, my cigarette case.*
> *To Maisie…*

The note stopped there. What did it mean? Rosemary wasn't going to die. She had been very ill, but she was better now.

'… my money goes to you anyway…'

Iris had always thought Uncle Paul's fortune would go to George if Rosemary died, but it said here that the money would come to her instead. That did make things rather less unfair… She was surprised by the thought. Had she felt it was unfair for Rosemary to get all Uncle Paul's money? Perhaps, deep in her heart, she had. Rosemary always had everything! Parties, pretty dresses, young men in love with her and an adoring husband.

Iris picked up the unfinished letter, and put it safely away in one the drawers of the desk. After the fatal birthday party, it was used to prove that Rosemary had been depressed after her illness, and might have been considering suicide. Depression after influenza was the <u>verdict</u> given at the <u>inquest</u>[3].

Now, Iris wondered how she had not been able to see the truth.

◆ ◆ ◆

After Rosemary's funeral the family lawyer had explained the details of Paul Bennett's will to Iris. Rosemary had <u>inherited</u>

his fortune, and she was meant to pass it on to her own children when she died. But if she died childless, the money would go to Iris when she reached the age of twenty-one, or when she got married[2].

George invited Iris to continue living with him. He suggested that her aunt, Mrs Lucilla Drake, should also come and live with them[4]. Mrs Drake had very little money of her own because her son spent it all, and so she was very pleased by George's invitation. Iris had happily agreed to the arrangement. George treated her like a younger sister, and Mrs Drake, who was a rather silly woman, let her do just as she pleased. The new household settled down comfortably together.

Six months after Rosemary's death, Iris had gone up into the attic of the house to look for a favourite jumper, which was packed away in a suitcase of clothes she did not wear. Searching through the suitcase, she found an old robe that had belonged to Rosemary, and felt something in one of the pockets. She reached into the pocket and pulled out a letter in Rosemary's handwriting.

Darling, I know you don't mean it… We love each other! We can't just say goodbye. We belong together – for ever and ever! I don't care what people say. Love matters more than anything. You once said that life was nothing without me. And now you say that our relationship must end. But I can't live without you – can't, can't, CAN'T! George will understand that it isn't right to live together if you don't love each other any more. We'll be wonderfully happy, darling, but we must be brave. I shan't tell George until after my birthday. Oh, darling

The letter ended here. So, Rosemary had had a lover. And she had planned to go away with him. Who was this unknown man? Did he love Rosemary as much as she loved him? He must have done. And yet, he had suggested ending it. Was he tired of her? It seemed that he had wanted to end the affair, but that Rosemary had disagreed...

Rosemary had had many <u>admirers</u>, but there had been no one special, had there? Iris <u>frowned</u>. Could it have been Stephen Farraday? People said he was a brilliant politician – a possible future Prime Minister! Was that the attraction? Surely Rosemary couldn't really have loved such a cold, unemotional man? But it must be Stephen Farraday. Because, if it wasn't, it had to be Anthony Browne. And Iris didn't want it to be Anthony Browne.

Anthony had been devoted to Rosemary, but he had disappeared after her death, and no-one had seen him since. Of course, he travelled a lot. He had mentioned South America, Canada, Uganda and the USA. Iris thought he was actually American, although his accent was very slight. And there was no reason why he should have continued to visit the rest of them. He was Rosemary's friend, after all. But Iris didn't want him to have been Rosemary's lover. That would hurt – terribly.

She wanted to throw the letter away, but something stopped her from doing it. One day it might be necessary to show someone that letter, to explain why Rosemary killed herself. So instead, she took it downstairs, and locked it in her jewellery box.

◆ ◆ ◆

Rosemary had died in November. In May, Iris, assisted by her Aunt Lucilla, had entered London's social world[5]. She went to lunches, teas and dances, but she didn't enjoy them very much.

It was at a rather boring dance at the end of June that she had heard someone behind her say 'Iris Marle?'

She had turned round, and looked straight into Anthony Browne's handsome face.

'You probably don't remember me,' he said, 'but…'

'Of course I do!' she smiled.

'Oh, that's <u>splendid</u>. It's been such a long time since I saw you.'

'I know. Not since Rosemary's birthday par—' She stopped in distress. (Rosemary's birthday party. Rosemary's suicide. She wouldn't think of it. She would *not!*)

'I'm terribly sorry,' he said, quickly. 'I shouldn't have reminded you.'

Iris swallowed hard. 'It's all right.'

'Please forgive me. Shall we dance?'

She nodded and floated onto the dance floor in his arms. 'Where have you been all this time?' she heard herself asking.

'Travelling, on business.'

'I see. So, why have you come back now?'

He smiled. 'To see you, Iris Marle.'

Since then, Iris had seen Anthony at least once a week. She walked with him in the park, sat next to him at dinner parties, danced with him[6]. But he never came to Elvaston Square, always cleverly managing to avoid accepting her invitations. She began to wonder why. Was it, perhaps, because he and Rosemary had been lovers there in the past?

Then, one day, George had suddenly questioned her about the relationship. 'Who's this Anthony Browne you're seeing?' he asked. 'What do you know about him?'

She stared at him in surprise. 'Tony? He was a friend of Rosemary's.'

George blinked. 'Oh, yes, of course he was. Well, you should be careful of the <u>fellow</u>. You're a very rich young woman, you know.'

'Tony has plenty of money,' she cried, angrily. 'Why, he's staying at Claridge's hotel!'

George smiled. 'Very respectable – and expensive! All the same, my dear, nobody knows much about him. He doesn't come to this house, does he?'

'No. And I can see why, if you're so <u>horrid</u> about him!'

'I'm simply warning you. I'll talk to Lucilla.'

George did mention Anthony Browne to Aunt Lucilla, but she did not pay much attention to him at the time because her attention was focused on a <u>telegram</u> from her <u>beloved</u> son in Rio de Janeiro. *'Can you send me two hundred pounds?'* it said. *'Life or death. Victor'*

'Victor knows I don't have much money, so he wouldn't ask for help unless it was an emergency. I'm so afraid he'll shoot himself. I would never forgive myself if I didn't do what he asked.'

George sighed. 'I'll find out exactly what sort of trouble Victor's in. But you should let him try to get out of trouble by himself, Lucilla. He'll never take any responsibility for himself otherwise.'

'You're cruel, George. The poor boy has always been unlucky...'

George kept his thoughts about Victor to himself and decided to ask his efficient secretary to deal with it. He simply said, 'I'll get Ruth to send a telegram at once. We should know by tomorrow.'

The two hundred pounds was eventually reduced to fifty, which George paid himself. Iris told George how much she admired his kindness.

'Well, there's always one <u>loser</u> in the family,' he said, 'who must be supported by the others.'

'But Victor isn't *your* family. Couldn't *I* do it? You're always saying how rich I am.'

He smiled. 'Not until you're twenty-one. And I hope you won't do it then. But I'll give you one piece of advice. When someone threatens to end his life unless he gets two hundred pounds at once, twenty pounds will usually be enough... and ten will do! You can always cut down the amount. Victor would never kill himself! The people who threaten suicide never do it.'

'Never? What about Rosemary?' thought Iris.

◆ ◆ ◆

Since Rosemary's death, George seemed older, and heavier. He had grown increasingly <u>absent-minded</u>, and spent a lot of time deep in thought. Something serious seemed to be worrying him. Iris sometimes noticed him staring at her with a puzzled look on his face. Then he started returning early from work and going straight into his study. She had followed him in there one afternoon, and found him sitting at his desk, staring into space. When she asked him what the matter was, he replied quickly, 'Nothing.'

As time went on, he began to ask peculiar questions, such as, 'Iris, did Rosemary ever talk to you?'

'Of course, George. About what?'

'Oh, herself, her friends. Whether she was happy. That sort of thing.'

Iris was afraid that George had found out about Rosemary's affair. But she didn't want to hurt him, and Rosemary had never *said* anything – so she shook her head.

'Oh, well, it doesn't matter,' he sighed.

Another day he asked her who Rosemary's best friends had been.

'Gloria King and Maisie Atwell,' she replied.

'Would she have told her secrets to them?'

'I don't know. What sort of secrets do you mean?'

'Well, was she afraid of anybody? Did she have any enemies?' Iris stared at him in astonishment, and his face turned red. 'I just wondered.'

The next day, he asked her how well Rosemary knew the Farradays.

'I really don't know, George. But she was interested in politics.'

'Only after she met the Farradays in Switzerland. She never thought about political matters before that.'

'I think Stephen Farraday got her interested in the subject.'

'What did Sandra Farraday think about that? She might <u>resent</u> him having a friendship with another woman.'

Iris felt uncomfortable. 'Perhaps,' she agreed.

George suddenly changed the subject. 'Are you still seeing Anthony Browne?'

'Yes.'

'Isn't his business something to do with <u>armaments</u>?'

'He has never said.'

'Well, he certainly spent a lot of time with <u>Lord</u> Dewsbury last year, and Dewsbury is the chairman of United Arms Ltd. Rosemary saw a lot of Browne, too, didn't she? He took her dancing.'

'Yes.'

'I was surprised that she wanted him at her birthday party, though. She hadn't known him for long.'

'He dances very well...' A picture of the fatal party at the Luxembourg restaurant flashed across Iris's mind. The round table, the soft lights, the seven guests: herself, Anthony, Rosemary, Stephen Farraday, Ruth Lessing, George and Stephen's wife Lady Alexandra, known to her friends as Sandra. That was the first time Iris had met Tony properly. Before then, he had just been a name, a shadow in the hall waiting to <u>escort</u> Rosemary out to yet another party ...

She pulled her mind back into the present, to hear George saying, 'Well, do ask Browne to dinner one night, my dear. I'd like to meet him again.'

Iris was delighted. She gave George's invitation to Tony and he accepted, but on the day of the dinner he suddenly had to leave London on a business matter, and couldn't come after all.

◆ ◆ ◆

In July, George announced that he had bought a house called Little Priors, in the Sussex countryside.

'Will it need decorating?' asked Mrs Drake.

'Oh, Ruth is arranging all that for us.'

Ruth Lessing, George's efficient secretary, was pleasant, and good-looking in a hard, black-and-white kind of way. George was devoted to her, and relied on her completely.

Lucilla Drake was annoyed. 'George, dear, women do like to arrange the colour scheme of their own drawing room!'

George looked upset. 'I wanted it to be a surprise!'

'I'm sure Ruth will have made it perfect,' said Iris. 'She's so clever. What shall we do down there? Is there a tennis court?'

'Yes, and it's only fourteen miles to the sea. And we'll have neighbours we know, too. The Farradays own a house nearby.'

◆ ◆ ◆

They spent most of August and September in Sussex. Little Priors was a handsome house, with elegant furniture and decoration. Visitors came to stay at the weekends. There were tennis parties, and dinners with the Farradays. Sandra Farraday introduced them to the rest of their neighbours, and advised George about buying horses[7]. Stephen was often away in London, working on political business. Iris suspected that he was deliberately avoiding the family at Little Priors.

◆ ◆ ◆

The household had returned to London in October, and Iris had hoped that perhaps George would start behaving normally again. But then, late last night, he had knocked on her bedroom door, and asked her to come into his study for a talk. Half-asleep, she had agreed.

Downstairs, in the study, he invited her to sit down. 'Is anything the matter, George?' she asked, as he lit a cigarette with a shaking hand. He looked really ill.

'I can't go on alone. You must tell me if you think it's possible...' He rubbed his hand over his face. 'You'll understand when I've shown you these.' He handed Iris two neatly printed letters.

The first one said, 'YOUR WIFE DIDN'T COMMIT SUICIDE. SHE WAS KILLED.'

The second said, 'ROSEMARY WAS MURDERED.'

'They came about three months ago,' George continued. 'At first I thought it was a cruel joke, but then I began to think.

Why *would* Rosemary have killed herself? Lots of people have influenza and feel a bit depressed afterwards, but Rosemary wouldn't kill herself just because she was unhappy. She might threaten to, but she wouldn't actually do it.'

'But what other explanation could there be, George? They found the cyanide poison in her handbag.'

'I know. But ever since these letters came, I've been thinking about it, and I believe they're true. That's why I asked you if Rosemary had enemies, or was afraid of anyone. Whoever killed her must have had a reason, and you must help me find out, Iris. You've got to remember that night in every detail. Because if she was killed, you see, the murderer must have been sitting at that table!'

CHAPTER 2
RUTH LESSING

Ruth Lessing, a well-dressed, dark-haired woman of twenty-nine, was devoted to George Barton. When she had first come to work for him, six years ago, at the age of twenty-three, she had discovered that he was a very disorganized man. Being a business-like young woman, she had immediately taken control of his affairs. She had saved him time and money, chosen his friends, and advised him on his business decisions. George, Rosemary and Iris all called her Ruth, and she spent a lot of time with them at the house in Elvaston Square.

Last year, in early November, not long before Rosemary's death, George had spoken to Ruth about Victor Drake. 'I want you to do a rather unpleasant job for me, Ruth,' he said, one morning.

She nodded.

'My wife's cousin, Victor Drake, is a very bad man. He has ruined his mother, Lucilla, who has given him almost all her savings. He was caught forging a cheque while he was at Oxford University, and the family sent him abroad. He has travelled all over the world, but he never makes a success of anything he does. He's in London at the moment and has written to ask for money. I've made an appointment to meet him at twelve o'clock today, at his hotel, and I want you to go in my place. I believe the matter can be kept absolutely business-like if it's managed by a third person.'

'What do you want me to offer him?'

'A hundred pounds in cash and a ticket to Buenos Aires. The money will be given to him as he gets on the boat.'

Ruth smiled. 'You want to be sure he actually leaves!'

'Indeed. Are you sure you don't mind doing this for me?'

'Of course not.'

'Here's his ticket. I've booked him onto the *San Cristobal*, which sails from Tilbury <u>docks</u> tomorrow.'

Ruth put the ticket into her handbag. 'Where do I meet him?'

'At the Rupert Hotel, Russell Square. My dear, what would I do without you?' George put a hand on her shoulder <u>affectionately</u>. 'You're the kindest, <u>dearest</u> girl in the world!'

♦ ♦ ♦

Victor Drake was a very attractive man, but Ruth could sense the cold, <u>calculating</u> personality hidden beneath his obvious charm.

He greeted her with delight. 'So *you've* brought George's message? What a wonderful surprise!'

Calmly, she made George's offer, and Victor agreed to the deal at once. 'A hundred pounds? Not bad – I would have taken sixty, but don't tell George! And who's coming to see me off on the *San Cristobal*? You, my dear? How delightful.' His dark eyes smiled in his suntanned face. 'You've been with Barton for six years, haven't you, Miss Lessing? And he wouldn't know what to do without you. Oh, yes, I know all about you, my dear.'

'How do you know?' asked Ruth sharply.

Victor smiled broadly. 'Rosemary told me.'

'Rosemary?'

'She was very nice to me. She gave me a hundred pounds, actually,' he laughed.

Although she disapproved of his bad behaviour, Ruth found herself laughing, too. 'That's too bad of you, Mr Drake.'

'Not at all. I'm a professional <u>beggar</u>, with an excellent technique. My mother, for example, will always send money if I send a telegram suggesting suicide.'

'You should be ashamed of yourself.'

'Oh, I am. I'm a bad man, Miss Lessing. But I do enjoy myself greatly. I've lived a very interesting life. I've been an actor, a shop–keeper, a waiter, a builder, a <u>porter</u>, and a circus assistant. I stood for President in a South American Republic. I've been in prison! And I've never done an honest job, or paid my own bills.'

Ruth knew she should be horrified. But Victor Drake managed to make evil seem amusing.

'And you're not so good yourself, Ruth!' He was looking at her closely now. 'You <u>worship</u> success. George shouldn't have married that little fool Rosemary. He would have done much better to marry you. Rosemary's lovely, but she's got no brains at all. She's the kind of woman that men always fall in love with, but never stay with. Now, you… Well, if a man fell in love with you, he would never grow tired of it.'

'But George wouldn't fall in love with me!' she cried.

'Oh, Ruth. If anything happened to Rosemary, George would marry you at once. You know that as well as I do. You could twist him round your little finger.'

It's true, thought Ruth, suddenly very angry. If it weren't for Rosemary, I could make George marry me.

Victor was watching her with amusement. He enjoyed putting ideas into people's heads. Or showing them the ideas that were already there…

◆ ◆ ◆

Soon after Ruth returned to work that afternoon, Rosemary had called her on the telephone.

'Oh, Ruth,' she said, '<u>Colonel</u> Race won't be here in time for my party, so ask George who he would like to invite instead. We need another man. There are four women coming. Iris, Sandra Farraday, and – I can't remember the other one.'

'I'm the fourth. You very kindly asked me.'

'Oh, of course – I'd forgotten!' Rosemary laughed, and ended the call.

At that moment Ruth Lessing realized that she hated Rosemary Barton. Hated her for being rich and beautiful and careless and stupid. She didn't need to work in an office. Everything had been handed to her <u>on a golden plate</u>. Love affairs, a devoted husband...

'I wish you were dead,' Ruth said to the silent telephone.

Chapter 3
Anthony Browne

Ruth Lessing, a well-dressed, dark-haired woman of twenty-
Anthony Browne knew he had been a fool to get involved with
Rosemary Barton. After all, he wasn't staying at Claridge's
hotel for pleasure – he was in London to work. But Rosemary
was beautiful enough to excuse the fact that he was ignoring
his business affairs for a little while. Luckily, his interest in her
soon began to fade, and he knew that it wasn't love after all. But
they could still have a good time together. Rosemary danced
wonderfully and whenever they went out, other men turned
round to stare at her. It was very pleasant, as long as you didn't
want to talk to her. She couldn't even listen intelligently. But he
had taken her out, danced with her, kissed her in taxis and was
on the way to making a bit of a fool of himself over her … until
that incredible day.

He remembered the eager look in her dark blue eyes as she
said softly, 'Anthony Browne is a nice name!'

'It's very respectable,' he replied, lightly. 'There was an <u>advisor</u>
to King Henry the Eighth called Anthony Browne.'

'But you must be from the Italian branch of the family.'

'Because of my brown skin? I had a Spanish mother.'

'Oh, that explains it, *Mr Anthony Browne.*'

'You're very fond of my name,' he laughed.

'Well, it's nicer than *Tony Morelli.*'

He couldn't believe it! He caught hold of her arm. 'Where
did you hear that name?' His voice was suddenly dangerous.
'Who told you?'

She laughed in delight at his reaction. 'Someone who
recognized you.'

'*Who?* This is serious, Rosemary!'

'My <u>wicked</u> cousin, Victor Drake.'

'I've never met him.'

'He probably wasn't using that name when you knew him. I expect he had chosen to give a false one, in order to save the family embarrassment.'

Anthony said slowly. 'I see. So, you mean that we met in prison, then?'

'Yes. I saw Victor recently, and I was telling him what a disgrace to the family he was when he smiled broadly and said, "You aren't so perfect yourself, <u>sweetheart</u>. I saw you last night dancing with a <u>chap</u> who calls himself Anthony Browne. In prison, we knew him as Tony Morelli".'

Anthony smiled. 'Well, I'd like to see him again. We ex-prisoners must <u>stick together</u>.'

'You're too late. He sailed to South America yesterday.'

'So you're the only person now who knows my guilty secret?'

Rosemary nodded. 'And I won't tell.'

'You had better not. You don't want your pretty face <u>slashed</u>, do you? There are people around who are very happy to ruin a girl's beauty. And murder doesn't only happen in books and films. It happens in real life, too.'

'Are you threatening me, Tony?'

'I'm warning you. Forget the name Tony Morelli – *do you understand?*'

'But I don't mind, Tony. It's exciting to meet a criminal. You shouldn't be ashamed.'

He looked at her coldly, wondering how he could ever have cared for her. She was just a silly girl with a pretty face. He would have to leave. He couldn't trust her to keep his secret.

She smiled her <u>enchanting</u> smile. 'Don't look so fierce. Will you take me to the Jarrows' dance next week?'

'I won't be here. I'm going away.'

'Not before my birthday party! You can't! I've been very ill and you mustn't upset me! You *must* come.'

He was going to refuse – but at that moment, through the open <u>parlour</u> door, he saw Iris Marle coming down the stairs. Tall and slim, with dark hair and grey eyes. And Anthony Browne changed his mind.

CHAPTER 4
STEPHEN FARRADAY

From an early age, Stephen Farraday had been determined to succeed in life. He was a quiet, well-behaved boy who worked hard enough at school to earn a place at Oxford University. He graduated at the age of twenty-two, leaving his college with a reputation as a clever public speaker, a talent for writing newspaper articles, some useful friends, and an ambition to work in politics. Naturally shy, he worked hard to develop an excellent social manner, with the occasional flash of brilliance, and soon people began to say, 'That young man will go far.' He joined the Conservative party[8], and was quickly elected to a <u>parliamentary seat</u>. As he proudly entered the House of Commons[9] for the first time, Stephen knew he had chosen the right career.

However, he soon realized that he was a very unimportant member of the government. How could he rise to a higher position? People didn't trust young politicians, so he needed something more than his own talents to help him. He needed the help of a powerful political family.

Marriage was the answer, he decided. Marriage to a well-connected woman, who would share his life and his ambitions; who would give him children and be proud of his success.

One day he was invited to a party at Kidderminster House, in Mayfair[10]. The Kidderminsters were one of the most powerful political families in England. Lord and Lady Kidderminster had five daughters, three of them beautiful. Stephen was leaning beside a window, about twenty minutes after arriving at the party, when he noticed a tall, fair girl standing by the refreshment table, looking rather lost. He recognized her as Lady Alexandra Hayle – the least attractive of the Kidderminster's five daughters.

She did not have the same style and confidence as her prettier sisters, and he could see that she was shy and uncomfortable.

Suddenly, Stephen recognized his chance!

He walked across to stand beside her at the table and picked up a sandwich. Then, turning to her, he said, 'Do you mind if I talk to you? I don't know many people here and I can see you don't either.'

As he had guessed, the girl was too embarrassed to tell him who she really was.

They began talking together. Stephen mentioned a play, which she had also seen, dealing with some aspect of the social services. Soon, they were deep in a discussion about politics.

Stephen was careful not to <u>overdo</u> things. When he saw Lady Kidderminster entering the room looking for her daughter, he said goodbye and left the party. He did not want to be introduced to her just yet.

For several days afterwards, he watched Kidderminster House, patiently waiting for the chance to see Lady Alexandra alone. He was rewarded one morning, when she came out with a small dog and walked towards Hyde Park.

Stephen hurried ahead, so that when Sandra entered through the park gates, he was already walking along the path towards her. As they passed one another, he stopped in delighted surprise. 'I say, what luck! I wondered if I'd ever see you again. I didn't tell you my name the other day. I'm Stephen Farraday – an unimportant Member of Parliament[11].'

She blushed, and said, 'I'm Alexandra – Sandra - Hayle.'

His reaction was perfectly judged – surprise, embarrassment, <u>dismay</u>. 'Lady Alexandra! Oh, dear! You must have thought I was so rude at the party! I should have known.'

'It doesn't matter, Mr Farraday,' she <u>reassured</u> him, quickly. 'Please, don't be upset. Why don't we walk down to the river?'

After that, they often met in the park. They discussed politics, and he discovered that she was an intelligent and sympathetic woman. They became friends, and soon Stephen was invited to dinner at Kidderminster House. That evening, he made a good impression on Lord and Lady Kidderminster, who described him as 'A useful young man to know.'

Two months later Stephen proposed to Sandra. 'Sandra, I love you, and I want you to marry me. I believe that I shall be a very successful man one day. You won't be ashamed of your choice, I promise.'

'I'm not ashamed!'

'Then you do care for me, darling?'

'Didn't you know?'

'I had hoped – but I wasn't sure. I've loved you since I first saw you across the room and came over to speak to you. I was never more terrified in my life.'

'I think I loved you then, too...'

Sandra's parents were not happy that she wanted to marry a man from an ordinary family, who held an unimportant parliamentary position, but Lord Kidderminster knew his quiet daughter's determined nature. If she wanted Farraday, she would have him!

'The fellow has got a <u>promising</u> career ahead of him,' he admitted. 'And the Conservative party could certainly do with some young and talented new members[8].'

Lady Kidderminster agreed, <u>reluctantly</u>. 'Then we will have to help him ...'

So, Alexandra Hayle married Stephen Farraday, and they moved into a charming house in Westminster. Soon afterwards, Sandra's godmother died and left her a delightful old house in the country, called Fairhaven. Stephen returned to Parliament with new energy. His connection with the Kidderminsters promised him a rapid rise in his career, and his wife was the perfect partner he had imagined, his ideal companion. Life was turning out just as he had planned. At thirty-two, success already lay within his reach.

And then the Farradays took a holiday in St Moritz, a skiing resort in the Swiss Alps, and Stephen saw Rosemary Barton in the hotel. And the lie he had told to his wife became the truth at last. Across a room, he fell deeply, crazily, desperately in love. He had always believed that he was not a passionate man. Sensual pleasure held little interest for him. So, to fall in love like an inexperienced boy was a terrible shock. He could think of nothing but Rosemary's lovely face, her red-gold hair, her perfect figure. He couldn't eat or sleep. They went skiing together, danced together – and as he held her in his arms, he wanted her more than anything on earth.

Two weeks after they returned to London, he became Rosemary's lover. Their mad affair lasted for six months. Stephen worked at the House of Commons, spoke at political meetings, and thought only of Rosemary – their secret meetings, her warm embrace. It was a sensual, feverish dream.

And after the dream, he suddenly woke up. It was like coming out of a tunnel into daylight. One day he was a passionate lover, the next day he was Stephen Farraday again, thinking that perhaps they shouldn't meet quite so often. They had taken some serious risks. What if Sandra guessed the truth? Some of his excuses for absence lately had been pretty weak. Most women would have become suspicious by now.

He needed to escape.

He took a few days off work, and went down to Fairhaven with Sandra. It was peaceful, sitting in the gardens with his wife, playing golf, walking in the countryside. He felt like he was recovering from an illness.

He had told Rosemary not to write to him in Sussex. It was too dangerous, even though Sandra never asked him who his letters were from. So, when he recognized Rosemary's writing on an envelope at the breakfast table, he frowned, annoyed, and took it into his study to read.

Over several pages, Rosemary had written that she <u>adored</u> him, loved him more than ever, couldn't bear not to see him for five whole days. He thought that it was sweet of her to write, but she shouldn't have done it. Why couldn't she wait until he got back to London?

Another letter arrived the next morning. This time Stephen thought Sandra's eyes rested on it for a couple of seconds. But she didn't say anything. After breakfast he drove to the nearest town, to call Rosemary from a public telephone box.

'Hello, Rosemary?'

'Stephen, darling! Oh, I have missed you. Have you missed me?'

'Yes, of course. But don't write to me any more. It's not safe.'

'Don't be silly, darling. What does it matter?'

'I'm thinking of you, too, Rosemary.'

'Oh, I don't care what happens to me!'

'Well, I care, sweetheart.'

'When are you coming back?'

'Tuesday.'

'Can't you make an excuse and come up today?'

'I'm afraid it isn't possible.'

When Stephen rang off he felt exhausted. Rosemary and he must be more careful in future.

After that, things began to get difficult. Stephen was working so hard that it was impossible to give much time to Rosemary. But she didn't understand. She wasn't interested in his career. She just wanted him to tell her again and again that he loved her. Surely, he thought, she must know that by now! She made sudden, impossible demands. Couldn't he go down to the South of France and she could meet him there? One of those places where you never saw anyone you knew? Stephen said that there was no such place in the world. At the most unlikely spots you always met some old school friend that you hadn't seen for years.

'Well, it wouldn't really matter, would it?' she said.

He felt suddenly cold. 'What do you mean?'

She smiled at him. 'Darling, it's stupid to go on trying to keep this a secret, so let's stop pretending. George will divorce me and your wife will divorce you and then we can get married.'

Disaster! Ruin! 'I wouldn't let you do such a thing,' he said.

'But, darling, it doesn't matter what other people think of us.'

'It matters to me, my dear. A scandal of that kind would destroy my career.'

'But there are hundreds of other things that you could do. And you don't need to do anything, anyway! I've got lots of money of my own. We could travel the world!'

Who on earth did she think he was? At that moment, the <u>spell</u> was finally broken. Rosemary had a beautiful face and the brains of a chicken! And if Stephen wasn't careful, she would ruin his life. He said the things that men always say in these situations. They must end it <u>for her sake</u>. He couldn't risk making her unhappy.

But she had replied that she adored him! She couldn't live without him! They must tell the truth! She would tell George, and George would divorce her. Sandra would divorce Stephen, too – he had no doubt about that. And his career would not survive the scandal. Everything ruined because of his <u>lust</u> for a silly woman. He would lose everything. He would lose Sandra...

With a shock of surprise, Stephen realized that losing Sandra was his greatest fear. His dear, loyal Sandra. *No!* Somehow, he must keep Rosemary quiet.

'I won't do anything until after my birthday,' Rosemary had said. 'It would be too cruel. Dear George is making such a fuss about it.'

But if Stephen told her clearly that he no longer loved her, she might very well go to George in <u>hysterics</u>. She might even go to Sandra. He could hear Rosemary saying, through her tears, *'He says he doesn't care any more, but he's just being loyal to you. I know you'll agree that when people love each other, honesty is the only way. So, I'm asking you to give him his freedom.'*

And Sandra *would* free him. She wouldn't believe that Stephen truly loved her. How could she, if Rosemary showed her the letters he had been stupid enough to write. He had never written such letters to Sandra...

'It's a pity that we don't live in the days of the Borgias[12],' he thought. A glass of poisoned champagne was about the only thing that would keep Rosemary quiet.

And then, a week later, there was cyanide in Rosemary's champagne glass. And across the table, his eyes met Sandra's...

CHAPTER 5
ALEXANDRA FARRADAY

Sandra Farraday had loved Stephen from the moment he first spoke to her at Kidderminster House, pretending not to know who she was. She had realized that he *had* known, soon after their marriage. One day, when he was describing a clever piece of political strategy, she had recognized the same tactics he had used to win her.

She had always accepted that he did not love her in the same fierce way that she loved him. She thought that he wasn't actually capable of it. But she understood the job he wanted her to do. He needed her practical help, her brains and her connections. He didn't want her heart. But she knew that he liked her and enjoyed her company. So she hid her passionate devotion from him, and looked forward to a future full of friendship and affection.

And then Stephen met Rosemary Barton in St. Moritz.

Sandra wondered how he could imagine that she didn't know about them. She had known from the moment he first looked at the woman. She had known the very day the woman became his mistress. She knew the perfume the woman used…

Her pride had protected her. She would never show that she was hurt, never beg, never protest. And she had one small piece of comfort – Stephen didn't want to leave her. She knew that it was only for the sake of his career, but he wouldn't leave. And some day, the affair would end. Never for one minute did Sandra think of leaving him. Stephen was her life, her whole existence.

What did he see in the girl? She was very beautiful – but she was also silly and stupid. Sandra believed that Stephen would get tired of Rosemary in time. His main interest in life was his work. He had a fine political brain and was destined for great things. Surely once the attraction began to fade he would remember that fact?

When they went down to Fairhaven, Stephen had seemed more like himself, and hope rose in her heart. He still wanted her close to him, and asked for her advice. For the moment, he had escaped from that woman. If only he would end the affair...

Then they went back to London and it all began again. Stephen looked tired and ill. He couldn't concentrate on his work. Sandra thought she knew why. He was deciding to destroy everything he cared about most. It was madness! But Stephen would not be the first man who had <u>sacrificed</u> his career for a beautiful woman and been sorry afterwards.

How beautiful Rosemary had looked that night at the Luxembourg, as she stood before the mirror in the ladies' cloakroom, fixing her make-up. She looked thin and pale after her recent illness. 'Oh, this horrid flu has exhausted me,' she <u>exclaimed</u>. 'I look awful. And I still feel weak and have a headache. You haven't got an <u>aspirin</u>, have you, Sandra?'

'No, but I've got a <u>sachet</u> of headache powder.' Sandra had taken the paper packet from her handbag and given it to Rosemary, just as Ruth Lessing came up to take her place at the mirror. Then they had gone out to join the men in the hall: Sandra, Rosemary, Ruth Lessing, and Rosemary's sister, Iris. As they walked into the dining room, there had been no warning that one of them would never go through that <u>doorway</u> again, alive...

Chapter 6

George Barton

George Barton had always been crazy about Rosemary, but when he asked her to marry him, he thought she would just laugh at him. After all, he knew she didn't love him. To his amazement, however, she accepted his offer.

'I know I will feel settled and happy and safe with you. I'm sick of being in love. It always goes wrong. I like you, George. You're funny and sweet and you think I'm wonderful. That's what I want.'

Amazed and delighted by her unexpected decision, George had answered in an uncertain voice, 'We'll be as happy as kings.'

And they had been happy. George had always known that Rosemary wouldn't be content with a dull man like him, that she would have affairs. But he knew that she would always come back to him. Her affection for him existed quite separately from her love affairs. He had not minded her <u>flirtations</u> with various young men, but when she began a serious affair, he discovered that it was a different matter. He had known immediately, sensing her excitement. And on the day when he had gone into her sitting room and she had quickly covered up the letter she was writing, he had guessed she was writing to her lover. When she left the room, taking the letter with her, he crossed to the desk and picked up the <u>blotting paper</u> she had used to dry the ink on the page. He had held it up to the mirror on the wall and read the words,

My own beloved darling…

A wave of anger had swept over him. Who was it? That fellow Browne? Or Stephen Farraday? They had both been flirting with her. He had caught sight of his reflection in the mirror. His eyes were red. He looked as if he was about to collapse.

Well, he would never suffer like that again. Rosemary had been dead for nearly a year now, and so they were both at peace. And it was time to concentrate on his plan. He would speak to Colonel Race first, and see what he thought of the <u>anonymous</u> letters. And then... He had it all worked out. The date: November 2nd, which was <u>All Souls' Day</u>. That was a clever detail. The place: The Luxembourg. The same table, and the same guests; Anthony Browne, Stephen and Sandra Farraday, Ruth, Iris and himself. He would also invite Race, who had been invited to the original dinner, but had been unable to attend. And there would also be one extra, empty place.

BOOK 2
ALL SOULS' DAY

-------------------- CHAPTER 1 --------------------

It was late October and at Little Priors, George Barton's country house, Lucilla Drake was busy organizing the family's return from Sussex to London for the winter. As she considered the many <u>housekeeping</u> matters that must be managed, she looked worriedly across at Iris, who was resting on a sofa. The girl seemed pale and tired.

'My dear, you look as though you haven't slept. You're black under the eyes. I think the air here is unhealthy. This house is in a <u>hollow</u>. If George had consulted me instead of Miss Lessing... It's a great mistake to encourage her to think herself one of the family.'

'But Aunt, Ruth *is* practically one of the family.'

Mrs Drake was not impressed. 'She intends to be, that's quite clear. But that's unacceptable. George must be protected, and I think you should tell him that marriage to Miss Lessing is out of the question.'

Iris was surprised. 'I had never thought of George marrying Ruth. Wouldn't it be rather nice? I think she would make him a very good wife.'

'George is very well looked after already! I am perfectly able to see to his comfort and his health. What does a young woman out of an office know about housekeeping?'

Iris smiled. Poor Aunt Lucilla. Romance was so far back in the past for her now that she had probably forgotten what it meant – if indeed, it had ever meant much.

Lucilla had been the half-sister of Iris and Rosemary's father, Hector. She was nearly forty when she met and married the elderly Reverend Caleb Drake, who died two years later, leaving her with a baby son. Being a mother had been the greatest experience of Lucilla Drake's life. Her son Victor had turned out to be a problem – but she refused to see anything wrong in him except a slight weakness of character. She thought her dear boy was too trusting, too easily influenced by bad friends. He was unlucky. He was too innocent and therefore deceived by wicked men. She knew how much Victor hated asking her for money. But when the poor boy was really in trouble, who else could he ask?

George's invitation to come and live with him and Iris had come at a moment when she had been in danger of real poverty. She had been happy and comfortable with them and did not like the thought of being replaced by a young woman, who, she believed, would only be marrying George for his money. Thank goodness there was at least one person who could see what Ruth Lessing was planning to do!

CHAPTER 2

'I wish they had never come to Little Priors,' Sandra exclaimed bitterly, as George and Iris left Fairfield after having lunch with the Farradays.

Stephen turned to look at her in surprise. 'I didn't know you felt like that about them, too,' he said.

'Neighbours are different in the country. You have to be either friends or enemies; you can't just see people occasionally, as you can in London. And so now we've got to go to this extraordinary party.'

They were both silent, remembering the scene at lunch, where George Barton's behaviour had been noticeably strange. He had been extremely friendly, but there had been a clear <u>undercurrent</u> of excitement in him. And then – that sudden, unexpected invitation. A party for Iris's eighteenth birthday. He did hope the Farradays would both come. Stephen and Sandra had been so kind to them here in Sussex. He had insisted on setting the date right then.

'I thought perhaps one day the week after next – Wednesday or Thursday? Thursday is November 2nd. Would that be all right? But we'll arrange any day that suits you both.'

It was an invitation that you couldn't politely refuse. Stephen had noticed Iris Marle blushing with embarrassment as Sandra smilingly accepted and said that Thursday, November 2nd, would suit them very well.

Now, voicing his thoughts, Stephen said sharply, 'We don't have to go. We can make some excuse.'

Sandra turned to look at him. 'He'll just change the date. He seems very anxious for us to come.'

'I can't think why. It's Iris's party, and I doubt she particularly wants us there.'

'No.' Sandra sounded thoughtful. 'You know this party is to be at the Luxembourg?'

'But that's ridiculous.' He was shocked. 'The man must be mad! We will certainly refuse to go. The whole thing with Rosemary's death was terribly unpleasant. The publicity, the pictures in the papers! Doesn't he realize how unpleasant it would be for us?'

'George told me his reason, Stephen. He said that Iris has avoided the Luxembourg ever since that night. But he consulted a psychiatrist, who said that after a bad shock, the cause of the trouble must be faced, not avoided. George believes it would help Iris forget all her unhappy memories if he planned a pleasant party at the same restaurant, with, as far as possible, the same guests at the table.'

'How delightful!' Stephen observed. He was actually horrified by the thought.

'Do you really mind, Stephen?'

'I think it's a rather nasty idea. But if *you* don't mind—'

'I do mind, very much. But George made it impossible to refuse.'

'You don't have to go. *I'll* go and you can cancel at the last minute with a headache, or something.'

Sandra lifted her chin. 'That would be cowardly. No, Stephen, if you go, I go. After all,' she laid her hand on his arm, 'however little our marriage means, it should at least mean sharing our difficulties.'

He stared her in horror. 'Why do you say that? *However little our marriage means?*'

She looked back at him calmly. 'Well, isn't it true?'

'*No!* A thousand times no! Our marriage means *everything* to me.'

She smiled. 'I suppose we do make a good partnership, don't we?'

'Of course we do – but that's not what I meant.' Stephen was finding it hard to breathe. He took her hand in both of his, holding it very tightly. 'Sandra,' he said, shaking, 'don't you know that you mean the world to me?' Then, suddenly she was in his arms and he was holding her close, and kissing her. 'Sandra – Sandra, darling! I *love* you! I've been so afraid I would lose you…'

'Because of Rosemary?' she asked.

'Yes.' He let her go, and stepped back, ashamed. 'You knew?'

'Of course.'

'And you understand?'

She shook her head. 'No. I don't think I ever will. Did you love her?'

'Not really. It was you I loved.'

'From the first moment you saw me across the room?' she reminded him, suddenly angry. 'Don't repeat that lie! For it *was* a lie.'

He answered, thoughtfully. 'Yes, it was – but I'm beginning to believe that it was actually true.'

'You were *not* in love with me,' she said, bitterly.

'I had *never* been in love. I was not a passionate man. I was even *proud* of my emotional control! And then I did fall in love "across a room", in St. Moritz. It was a silly, violent love like a summer storm – brief, false, and quickly over.' He paused. 'It was here, at Fairhaven, that I realized that your love was the only thing in life that mattered to me.'

'I thought you were planning to go away with her.'

'With Rosemary?' He gave a short laugh. 'That would have been <u>penal servitude</u> for life!'

'Didn't she want you to go away with her?'

'Yes, she did.'

'What happened?'

Stephen drew a deep breath. 'The Luxembourg happened.'

They both fell silent, remembering. Then Sandra asked, 'What are we going to do?'

'We'll face it together,' said Stephen, 'and go to this horrible party, whatever George's reason for it may be.'

'You don't believe his story about Iris?'

'No. Do you?'

'It could be true. But it's not the real reason.'

'What do you think this party is, Sandra?'

She met his eyes. 'I think it's a <u>trap</u>.'

CHAPTER 3

On the way back from lunch with the Farradays at Fairfield, Iris turned to George. 'Do you mind if I go for a walk? I've got an awful headache.'

'My poor child, of course. I won't come with you, though. I have a friend coming to visit me this afternoon.'

'Right, then. Goodbye till tea-time.'

Iris walked away through a wood and up a nearby hill. When she reached the top, she stopped and sat down on a fallen tree. The October afternoon was damp, and grey clouds promised more rain. She was looking down into the valley, when she heard a slight <u>rustle</u> in the trees behind her. Looking round, she saw Anthony Browne walking towards her. 'Tony!' she cried. 'How did you know where I was?'

He sat down and took out his cigarette case. 'I have an excellent pair of <u>binoculars</u>. I knew you were having lunch with the Farradays, so I spied on you from the hill and followed you when you left.' He smiled and lit his cigarette.

'Why didn't you come to the house like an ordinary person?'

'I'm not an ordinary person,' said Anthony in a shocked tone. 'I'm very extraordinary.'

'I think you are.'

He looked at her quickly. Then he said, 'Is anything the matter?'

'No. At least...' She drew a deep breath. 'I hate being down here. I want to go back to London.'

'You're going soon, aren't you?'

'Next week.'

'So this was a <u>farewell party</u> at the Farradays?'

'It wasn't a party. Just lunch.'

'Do you like the Farradays?'

'Not very much – although they've been very nice to us. Stephen always seems to me rather arrogant and stupid.'

'He's not stupid. He's just one of the usual unhappy successes.'

'Unhappy?'

'Most successes are unhappy. That's why they are successes – they have to reassure themselves about who they are by achieving something that the world will notice. The happy people are failures because they are so content in themselves that they don't care what other people think. Like me. They are also usually very pleasant company – again, like me.'

'You have a very good opinion of yourself.'

'I'm just drawing attention to my good points in case you haven't noticed them.'

Iris laughed, suddenly feeling much happier. She glanced at her watch. 'Come and have tea, and give a few more people the benefit of your pleasant company.'

Anthony shook his head. 'I can't stay long.'

'Why will you never come to the house?' she demanded. 'There must be a reason.'

Anthony <u>shrugged</u> his shoulders. 'George doesn't like me.'

'Why are you here then? Do you have business in this part of the world?'

'Very important business – with you. I came to ask you a question, Iris.' His eyes were very serious. 'Do you trust me? It's the most important question in the world to me. *Do you trust me?*'

After a brief moment she answered, 'Yes.'

'Then will you come up to London now and marry me, without telling anybody?'

She stared at him. '*I couldn't!*'

'You do love me, don't you?'

'Yes, Anthony,' she heard herself say.

'But you won't come and marry me by special licence at the Church of Saint Elfrida, in Bloomsbury?'

'I can't! George would be so hurt and Aunt Lucilla would never forgive me. And I'm not old enough anyway. I'm only eighteen. I can't marry without legal <u>consent</u> until I'm twenty-one[13].'

'You'd have to lie about your age.'

'But why? What's the point of it?'

'You have to trust my reasons. Let's say that it is the simplest way. But never mind.'

Iris said in a frightened voice, 'If George only knew you a little better... Come back with me now. It will only be him and Aunt Lucilla.'

'Are you sure? I thought I saw a man going up your <u>drive</u>. And I believe I recognized him as someone I – had met.'

'Oh, yes, I forgot. George was expecting someone.'

'The man I thought I saw was a man called Colonel Race.'

'It's very likely,' Iris agreed. 'George does know a Colonel Race. He was coming to dinner on that night when Rosemary...' She broke off, and drew a deep breath. 'Anthony, did you ever think that Rosemary might not have committed suicide? That she might have been murdered?'

'Good heavens, Iris – certainly not! What put such a thought into your head?'

She wanted to tell him the incredible story of George's anonymous letters, but instead she said slowly, 'It was just an idea.'

'Well, forget it, my darling.' He pulled her to her feet and kissed her lightly on the cheek.

CHAPTER 4

Colonel Race was a tall, military-looking man in his sixties, with a tanned face, short grey hair, and intelligent dark eyes. Race was twenty years older than George Barton, who he had known ever since George was a boy. They were not particularly close friends. Race was an outdoors type of man, who had spent most of his life abroad, working for British Intelligence, while George was definitely a city gentleman. At this moment, Race was wondering just why 'young George' had asked him to come down to see him in Sussex. George had always been a cautious, practical, sensible man. But this afternoon he seemed very nervous.

Race took his pipe out of his mouth and looked across at George. 'So, young George, what's the trouble?'

'I need your advice, Race — and your help. Almost a year ago you were invited to have dinner with us in London, at the Luxembourg, but you had to go abroad at the last minute.'

Race nodded. 'To South Africa.'

'At that dinner party, my wife died.'

'I know. I read about it. Didn't mention it now, or offer you sympathy, because I didn't want to upset you. But I am sorry, you know that.'

'Oh, yes, yes. But that's not the point. My wife was supposed to have committed suicide.'

Race's eyebrows rose. *'Supposed?'*

'Read these.' George handed the two letters to Race.

'Anonymous letters? Who do you think wrote them, George?'

'I don't know. I don't care. But I believe they're true. My wife was murdered.'

Race put down his pipe. 'Did you suspect this at the time? Did the police?'

'No, I just accepted the verdict. There was no suggestion of anything except suicide. The cyanide was in her handbag, so it seemed, at the time, quite straightforward.'

'Had she ever threatened to commit suicide?'

'Never. Rosemary loved life.'

Race had only met George's wife once. He had thought her beautiful but stupid – but not depressed. 'What was the medical evidence as to her state of mind?'

'Rosemary's own doctor was away on holiday at the time. His partner looked after Rosemary when she had the influenza, and he said it could cause serious depression. Later Rosemary's own doctor told me that he was very surprised at what had happened. Rosemary was not the type to commit suicide, he said.' George paused. 'It was then that I realized how unlikely Rosemary's suicide was. She could certainly get very emotional about things, and she would sometimes act without thinking, but I have never known her want to abandon life completely. What's more, if Rosemary *had* wanted to kill herself, she would never have done it that way. It was painful and... ugly. An <u>overdose</u> of sleeping medicine would be far more likely.'

'I agree. Was there any evidence as to how she obtained the cyanide?'

'No. But she had been staying with friends in the country and they had used cyanide to destroy a wasps' <u>nest</u>[1] there one day. It was thought that she might have taken some then.'

'So, there was no natural <u>disposition</u> to commit suicide, nor any preparation for it. But there can't have been any evidence for murder, or the police would have found it. They're quite clever, you know.'

'Just the idea of murder would have seemed incredible then.'

'But it didn't seem so to you six months later?'

George said slowly, 'I think I must have been <u>subconsciously</u> unhappy all along. So when I saw the thing written down, it made sense at once.'

Race nodded. 'So, who do you suspect?'

George looked ill. 'If Rosemary was killed, one of those people at the table, one of our friends, must have done it. No one else came near us.'

'Who poured the wine?'

'Charles, the head waiter at the Luxembourg.'

Everybody knew Charles. It was impossible to imagine that he would deliberately poison a client.

'And the waiter who served us was Giuseppe, who always looks after me there. He's a delightful fellow.'

'So who was at the dinner party?'

'Stephen Farraday, the MP. His wife, Lady Alexandra. My secretary, Ruth Lessing. A fellow called Anthony Browne. Rosemary's sister Iris, and myself. There should have been eight guests, but when you cancelled, we couldn't think of anyone else to ask at the last minute.'

'Where were you all sitting?

'I had Sandra Farraday on my right. Anthony Browne sat next to her. Then Rosemary, Stephen, Iris – and Ruth Lessing, who sat on my left.'

'Had your wife drunk champagne earlier in the evening?'

'Yes. The glasses had been filled up several times. It happened while we were all watching the <u>cabaret</u> show. Rosemary collapsed just before the lights were turned up again. The doctor said that death must have been almost immediate.'

'Well, when you first consider it, the murderer seems obvious. Stephen Farraday was on her right. Her champagne glass would be close to his left hand. It would be simple to drop the poison in as soon as the lights were turned down and people were watching the show. Those Luxembourg tables are big, and I don't think anybody else could have leaned across the table without being noticed, even if it was dark. Even the man on Rosemary's left would have needed to lean across her to put anything in her glass. There is one other possibility, but we'll take Farraday first. Is there any reason why he would want to kill your wife?'

George answered unwillingly. 'They had been... close friends. If Rosemary had rejected him, he might have wanted revenge.'

Race looked at his red face, and continued. 'Possibility Number 2 is that it was one of the women.'

'Why?'

'In a party of seven, with four women and three men, there will be times during the evening when three couples are dancing and one woman is left sitting alone at the table. Did you all get up to dance?'

'Yes.'

'Before the cabaret, can you remember who was sitting alone at any moment?'

George thought. 'Yes. Iris was left out the last time, and Ruth the time before.'

'When did your wife last drink champagne?'

'Let me see, she had been dancing with Browne, who is rather an energetic dancer. I remember her coming back quite thirsty and finishing the champagne in her glass. Then she danced with me. Farraday danced with Ruth, and Lady Alexandra with Browne. Iris stayed at the table. Immediately after that, it was the cabaret.'

'Did Iris inherit any money on your wife's death?'

'My dear Race – don't be absurd. Iris was devoted to Rosemary!'

'Never mind. She had the opportunity, and I want to know if she had the motive. Your wife was a rich woman. Did her money go to you?'

'No, it went to Iris, <u>in trust</u> until she's twenty one.' He explained Paul Bennett's will.

'The rich sister and the poor sister,' Race observed. 'Some girls might have resented that.'

'I'm sure Iris didn't.'

'Maybe not – but she certainly had a motive. Who else did?'

'Nobody. Rosemary didn't have an enemy in the world. I've been asking questions, trying to find out. I've even taken this house near the Farradays, so as to…' He stopped.

Race picked up his pipe and began to clean it out. 'You had better tell me, George.'

'What do you mean?'

'You're hiding something. You can protect your wife's name, or you can try to find out if she was murdered. But you can't do both.'

'All right,' said George, unhappily.

'Did your wife have a lover?'

'Yes.'

'Was it Stephen Farraday?'

'I don't know. It could have been him or Browne. I couldn't tell.'

'Tell me about Anthony Browne. I think I have heard the name before.'

'He's a good-looking, amusing chap, but nobody knows anything about him. He's supposed to be American, but he doesn't have much of an accent.'

'And you've no idea which of them it was?'

'No. I found her writing a love letter to someone, and I examined the blotting paper afterwards – but there was no name.'

'Well, Lady Alexandra has a motive, if her husband was having an affair with your wife. And so do Browne and Farraday, if they were having affairs they wanted to end. And so does Iris, because of the money. What about Ruth Lessing, your secretary? What sort of a girl is she?'

'She's the dearest girl in the world. Practically one of the family. I depend upon her in every way.'

Race made no comment, but mentally noted a definite motive for Ruth Lessing – an ambition to become the second Mrs Barton. Whether she wanted her employer's money, or she was genuinely in love with him, the 'dearest girl in the world' had a very definite reason for wanting to remove Rosemary Barton.

'I suppose it's occurred to you, George,' he said, gently, 'that you had a rather good motive yourself.'

George looked horrified. 'No! It wasn't like that between me and Rosemary. I adored her, and she was very fond of me, but I always knew I would have to accept her love affairs. It hurt when it happened, but I would never have harmed her. And, anyway, if I had done it, why would I <u>stir things up</u> again, after a verdict of suicide was passed? It would be madness.'

'Absolutely. I don't seriously suspect you, my dear chap. A successful murderer who got letters like these would just put them quietly in the fire. So, who does want to stir things up again? Who do you think wrote those letters, George?'

'Servants?' said George, uncertainly.

'If so, what servants, and what do they know? Did Rosemary have her own <u>maid</u>[14]?'

'No. At the time we had a cook, Mrs Pound, who is still with us, and a couple of maids who have both left since then.'

'Well, now, Barton, think very carefully. Rosemary is dead. You can't bring her back. Do you really want to know if she was murdered? It may mean a lot of unpleasant publicity, your wife's love affairs will be common knowledge…'

'I want the truth!' cried George.

'Well, in that case, you must take these letters to the police.'

'I'm not going to the police – I'm going to set a trap for the murderer! I'm going to have a party at the Luxembourg, and I want you to come, Race. The same guests will be there: the Farradays, Browne, Ruth, Iris, and myself.'

'What are you going to do?'

George laughed. 'That's my secret. I want you to come – and see what happens.'

Race spoke sharply. 'George, these dramatic <u>gestures</u> don't work. Go to the police. They're professionals.'

'So are you. That's why I want you there.'

'Because I've worked for the Secret Service?' Race shook his head. 'I'm sorry, but I don't like your plan and I won't play. Give it up, George, there's a good man. It won't work, and it could be dangerous.'

'It will be dangerous for somebody all right.'

Race sighed. 'Oh, well, don't say I haven't warned you.'

CHAPTER 5

The morning of November 2nd was wet and <u>gloomy</u>. Iris sat at the dining room table, pushing her food around her plate. George read his newspaper, while Lucilla wept into a handkerchief. 'Victor wouldn't say it was a matter of life and death if it wasn't,' she sobbed.

'I've said I'll see to it, Lucilla,' <u>snapped</u> George.

'I know. But a delay might be fatal. Your inquiries will take time, and he says he needs the money "without fail by the 3rd". Which is tomorrow.'

'Don't worry, Aunt,' said Iris. 'George'll fix it. He always does.'

George got up and touched Mrs Drake kindly on the back as he walked past her chair. 'Cheer up, my dear. I'll get Ruth to send a telegram immediately.'

Iris followed him out into the hall. 'George, shall we cancel the party tonight? Aunt Lucilla is so upset. Shouldn't we stay at home with her?'

'Certainly not! Why should that damned <u>villain</u> upset our lives? It's <u>blackmail</u>, and Lucilla's a fool. If Victor had been forced to save himself from disaster, just once, it would have done him a great deal of good. But I'll get something arranged before tonight so that she can go to bed happy.'

As he walked out of the front door, the hall telephone rang and Iris went over to answer it.

'Hello? Anthony!' She smiled in delight.

'The man himself. Have you been talking to George?'

'What do you mean?'

'Well, he insisted I come to your birthday party tonight. I thought perhaps you had something to do with it?'

'No...'

'What's the matter, darling? I can hear you sighing through the telephone.'

'It's nothing.'

'Tell me, my sweet.'

'I *can't!*'

'I'll see you tonight, then. I suppose George knows what he's doing, but it seems madness to me.'

They said goodbye and ended the call, and Iris returned to the dining room to reassure her aunt.

◆ ◆ ◆

George arrived at his office, and sent for Ruth Lessing at once. 'Trouble again, Ruth. Look,' he said as she arrived.

She took the telegram he held out. 'Victor Drake!'

'Yes, unfortunately it is from him. Wasn't it a year ago that we sent him to Buenos Aires?'

'It was October 27th.'

Ruth had a good reason for remembering. It was after returning from her meeting with Victor Drake that she had listened to Rosemary's careless voice on the telephone and realized that she hated her.

'We're lucky that he's lasted as long as he has out there,' George observed.

'Three hundred pounds is a lot of money.'

'Oh, he won't get that much. We'll make the usual investigations. Send Ogilvie a telegram.' Alexander Ogilvie was George's business agent in Buenos Aires.

'I'll do it at once.'

◆ ◆ ◆

Ruth returned to George's office after lunch, with bad news. 'I'm afraid that Victor has been stealing money. Mr Ogilvie has just telephoned to say that the senior partner in the firm has agreed not to <u>prosecute</u> Victor if he repays the money. The sum is one hundred and sixty-five pounds.'

'So Victor was hoping to profit by one hundred and thirty-five pounds?'

'I'm afraid so. I told Mr Ogilvie to go ahead and pay the money back. Was that right?'

'Personally I would be happy to send him to prison, but we must consider his mother. So, Master Victor wins as usual.'

'You're a very good man,' said Ruth.

Pleased, and embarrassed, he picked up her hand and kissed it. 'Dearest Ruth. What would I do without you?'

CHAPTER 6

George sighed with relief. They were all here drinking cocktails in the Luxembourg, safe in his trap. Stephen Farraday, tall and stiff. Sandra Farraday in a black <u>velvet</u> dress, and an <u>emerald</u> necklace. Ruth, also wearing black, her dark hair smooth and shining. Iris, pale and silent, in a simple green dress. And Anthony Browne, the last to arrive. Now, the play could begin…

They finished their drinks and Charles, the head waiter, led them to a group of three tables in the far corner of the room. There was a large one in the middle and a small one on each side. A foreign-looking man and a fair-haired woman were sitting at one of the small tables. Another couple, a young man and his girlfriend, sat at the other. The large table was reserved for Barton's party.

George organized their seats. 'Sandra, you sit here, on my right. Browne, next to Sandra. Iris on my left, then Farraday, then Ruth.' Between Ruth and Anthony was an empty chair. The table had been laid for seven. 'Colonel Race may be late. He said we shouldn't wait for him.'

Iris was sure George had deliberately separated her from Anthony. Clearly, he still didn't trust him. She looked across the table, and saw that Anthony was frowning at the empty chair beside him. 'I'm glad you've got another man, Barton,' he said. 'I may have to leave early. I've seen a man here that I know.'

George smiled. 'Mixing business with pleasure, Browne? Not that I've ever known exactly what your business is?'

Anthony replied calmly. 'Organized crime, Barton. Robberies arranged. Families visited at their private addresses.'

Sandra Farraday laughed. 'No, you're something to do with armaments, aren't you?'

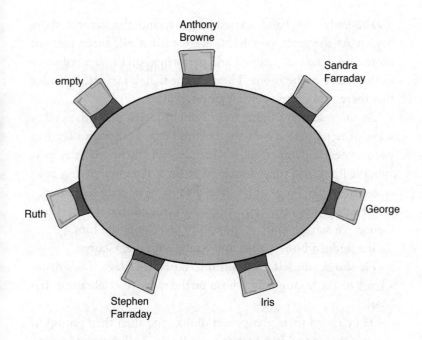

Anthony glanced at her in surprise. 'You mustn't <u>betray</u> my secrets, Lady Alexandra. There are spies everywhere!'

As the waiter removed their <u>oyster</u> plates, Stephen asked Iris to dance. Soon, everyone was dancing, and the party became more lively.

At last, it was Iris's turn to dance with Anthony. 'It's mean of George not to let us sit together,' she said.

'Not at all. This way I can gaze at you across the table.'

'Do you really have to go early?'

'I'm afraid so.'

When they returned to the table, there was a change in the atmosphere. All the guests seemed to feel the nervous tension in the air. Iris saw George glance at his watch.

Suddenly, the band started to play, and the cabaret show began. As the restaurant lights were turned off, three pairs of professional dancers entered and performed on the lighted stage in the centre of the room. Then a comedian did an act, and after that there was a display by a pair of <u>acrobats</u>.

As the restaurant lights were switched back on at the end, a wave of relief passed over the Barton table, as though they had been expecting something to happen, which had not. A year ago, the lights had turned back on to show Rosemary lying dead across the table. Now, at last, the shadow of tragedy had lifted.

Cheerful conversations began all round the table. Only George sat staring sadly at the empty place opposite him.

Iris <u>nudged</u> him. 'Come and dance with me, George.'

He shook himself and, smiling, raised his glass. 'Let's drink a <u>toast</u> to the young lady whose birthday we're celebrating. Iris Marle!'

They raised their glasses and drank, and then they got up to dance, George and Iris, Stephen and Ruth, Anthony and Sandra. When the dance ended, they all returned, laughing and talking.

Suddenly, George leaned forward. 'A year ago, we were here on an evening that ended in tragedy. I don't want to recall past sadness, but I don't want to feel that Rosemary is completely forgotten, so I'll ask you to drink to her memory.' He lifted his glass. 'To Rosemary.'

They all raised their glasses and drank the toast. There was a moment's pause, and then George collapsed in his chair, his hands at his throat, fighting for breath.

It took him a minute and a half to die.

BOOK 3
IRIS

·············· CHAPTER 1 ··············

Colonel Race met his old friend, Chief Inspector Kemp, at Scotland Yard[15].

'It was good of you to ring us, Colonel,' said Kemp, as they shook hands. 'We need all the help we can get on this case. The Kidderminsters are a powerful family. We mustn't upset them.'

'But what if Lady Alexandra or her husband murdered Barton?' asked Race.

Chief Inspector Kemp looked at him steadily. 'Then we'll hang him or her. But we'll have to be absolutely sure of our evidence.'

Race nodded. 'So, tell me what you know.'

'George Barton died of cyanide poisoning, just like his wife did a year ago. You say you were actually in the restaurant?'

'Yes. George had invited me to the party, but I refused. I didn't like what he was doing, trying to set a trap for the murderer, so I went along to the Luxembourg anyway, to keep an eye on things. I sat quite far away, so they wouldn't see me, and unfortunately, I saw nothing suspicious. The waiter and Barton's guests were the only people at the table.'

'I've got the waiter, Giuseppe Bolsano, here for questioning, but I can't believe he was involved.' Kemp shook his head. 'He has worked at the Luxembourg for twelve years and has a very good reputation.'

'Which leaves us with the guests.'

'The same people who were there when Mrs Barton died. The two deaths must be connected. Somebody told Mr Barton that his wife had been murdered, and he started to ask questions, so the murderer panicked and killed him, too. That seems to be what happened.'

'Yes,' agreed Race. 'We'll never know what George's "trap" at the dinner was going to be, because the killer didn't wait for it to happen.'

'So, we've got five <u>suspects</u> for this second murder.'

'Then you don't think Mrs Barton's death was suicide, after all?'

'There was some evidence for it at the time. A half-finished letter to the sister with instructions on how to give away her possessions, which showed suicide was in her mind. And she was certainly depressed, poor lady, but not necessarily because she had been ill. Usually, with women, it's because of a love affair.'

'You knew Mrs Barton was having a love affair?' asked Race, in surprise.

'Yes. It had been kept quiet, but it didn't take much to find it.'

'Was it with Stephen Farraday?'

'Yes. They used to meet in a little flat in Earl's Court. It had been going on for over six months. If they had had a fight, or if he was getting tired of her, well, she wouldn't be the first unhappy woman to kill herself.'

'By cyanide in a public restaurant?'

'If she wanted to be dramatic about it – and make him watch, too.'

'Did Farraday's wife know what was going on?'

'Not as far as we know.'

'But she might have done?'

'Oh, yes. Both the Farradays are possible murderers. She, because she was jealous. He, to protect his career.'

'What about the secretary, Ruth Lessing?'

'She might have been in love with Barton. His staff thought so. In fact, yesterday afternoon one of the office telephone girls was acting out Barton holding Ruth Lessing's hand and saying he couldn't do without her. Miss Lessing caught her doing it and dismissed her immediately, so she clearly felt sensitive about it. Then there's the sister, Iris, who inherited a fortune. And Mrs Barton's other boyfriend, Anthony Browne.'

'What do you know about him?'

'Not much. He's an American citizen, who works in the armaments trade. He's been staying at Claridge's hotel, where he met Lord Dewsbury. Dewsbury liked him and invited Browne to stay with him, and showed him round his factories. Soon after Browne's visit they found that some <u>tanks</u> had been <u>sabotaged</u>. Browne also made friends with Dewsbury's business partners, who showed him a lot of <u>classified</u> things he should never have seen. Several times there's been serious trouble at the factories soon after he left.'

'But why would Mrs Barton be a threat to him? George Barton wasn't connected to the armament world, was he?'

'No. But they were close friends, and he might have told her something important. You, of all men, know what a pretty woman can learn from a man, Colonel.'

Race nodded, knowing the Chief Inspector was referring to his work for the Secret Service, and not to his private affairs. 'Have you examined the letters that George Barton received?'

'Yes. Miss Marle gave them to me yesterday. Cheap paper, ordinary ink. No suspicious <u>fingerprints</u>.'

'And written by someone who had suspicions, but told George instead of the police. He couldn't have written them himself, could he, Kemp? To make his own suicide look like murder.'

'And so send Stephen Farraday to the <u>hangman's rope</u>? He would have needed to be certain that everything pointed to Farraday as the murderer, then. But we haven't got any evidence against Farraday at all. Cyanide was found in a small paper sachet under the table that night, but there were no fingerprints on it.'

'Did anybody notice anything helpful last night?'

'I took a brief statement from everyone last night, and then I went back to Elvaston Square with Miss Marle and had a look through Barton's desk. I will get more detailed statements from them today, and also from the people sitting at the tables on both sides.' He picked up a list. 'Gerald Tollington, of the Grenadier Guards, and the Honorable Patricia Brice-Woodworth – I'll bet that young couple didn't see anything but each other. And Pedro Morales – he's a rather unpleasant Mexican businessman – and his guest, Miss Christine Shannon. It's unlikely that any of them saw anything, but we'll have to check.'

CHAPTER 2

Giuseppe Bolsano was a small, middle-aged man, with an intelligent face. His English was fluent since he had, he explained nervously, been in the country since he was sixteen and had married an English wife.

'Now then, Giuseppe,' said Kemp, 'what else can you tell us about last night? What kind of champagne did they drink?'

'Clicquot, 1928,' said the little Italian waiter. 'A very expensive wine. Mr Barton liked the best.'

'And the empty place at the table?'

'Mr Barton told me that a young lady would occupy it later in the evening.'

'A young *lady?* 'Do you know who she was?'

Giuseppe shook his head.

'How many bottles of champagne did Mr Barton order?'

'Two. They finished the first one quite quickly, and I opened the second just before the cabaret began. I filled up the glasses and put the bottle in the ice bucket.'

'When did you last notice Mr Barton drinking from his glass?'

'When the cabaret ended, they drank a toast to the young lady. Then they all went to dance. When they returned to the table, Mr Barton drank again, and in a minute – like that! – he was dead.'

'Did you fill up the glasses while they were dancing?'

'No, Signore. There was still plenty left.'

'Did *anyone* come near the table while they were dancing?'

'No.'

'And they all returned from the dance floor at the same time?'

Giuseppe tried to remember. 'Mr Barton came back first, with the young lady. He did not want to dance for so long. Then came Mr Farraday, and the young lady in black. Lady Alexandra and the dark-haired gentleman came last.'

'If one of them had put something in Mr Barton's glass, would you have seen?'

'I cannot say, sir. I was serving all three tables in that corner, and two more in another part of the restaurant. After the cabaret, when everyone went to dance, I was just standing and watching, so I know that no one approached the table then. But when they sat down again, I was at once very busy. But it would be very difficult to do it without being observed, I think. Only Mr Barton himself could do it.'

'Is that what you think?' said Kemp.

'A year ago, the beautiful Mrs Barton killed herself. Perhaps Mr Barton was so unhappy that he decided to kill himself the same way?'

Kemp shook his head. 'I don't think it's that simple.'

Giuseppe was allowed to leave, and as the door closed behind him, Race said, 'I wonder if that's what we're meant to think?'

'Grieving husband kills himself on the anniversary of wife's death? Not that it was the anniversary – but near enough.'

'It was All Souls' Day – the day we remember the dead.'

'True. Well, possibly that was the idea. If so, the murderer can't have known about the letters that Mr Barton had shown to you and Iris Marle.' Kemp looked at his watch. 'I'm going to Kidderminster House at 12.30, but there's time to go and see the people at the other two tables first. Would you come with me, Colonel?'

CHAPTER 3

Mr Morales was staying at the Ritz. He was not a pretty sight. He had not shaved his chin, his eyes were red, and he had every sign of heavy drinking the night before. He said he was happy to help Chief Inspector Kemp and Colonel Race if he could, but he couldn't remember much about last night.

They asked what he could remember about the large table next to his own.

'I don't remember much about the people sitting there. At least not until that guy dropped dead. I do remember one of the ladies, though. Dark hair, black dress, great figure!' It was Ruth Lessing who had caught Mr Morales' attention. 'And, oh boy, she could really dance!'

Mr Morales admitted that he had been quite drunk by the time the cabaret began, and it was clear that he had no useful information to offer them. So Kemp thanked him and turned to leave the room.

'I'm sailing to New York tomorrow,' said Morales. 'Do you need me here? I'm enjoying myself, and if the police wanted me to stay in London, my boss won't complain.'

'Thank you, but I don't think your evidence will be needed at the inquest.'

◆ ◆ ◆

Kemp and Race next went to call on the Honourable Patricia Brice-Woodworth, in Brook Street.

'It's so annoying!' said Patricia, when they explained the reason for their visit. 'Probably the only chance in my life to be right there when a murder was done, and I wasn't even looking!'

As the Chief Inspector had guessed, Patricia and her fiancé Gerald, had only been interested in each other. 'And you'll find,' he said, angrily, as they left the house, 'that Gerald Tollington's story will be the same. Oh, well. Let's try Morales' dinner guest, Christine Shannon. Then we'll have finished with the extra witnesses.'

◆ ◆ ◆

Christine Shannon was extremely good to look at, and although she wasn't very intelligent, she had a lot of common sense and a talent for getting money from the men she attracted. She welcomed the two men into her small flat with real delight. 'I'd love to help you, Chief Inspector. Please, ask me anything you like.'

Kemp questioned her about the people at the large table, and she proved to be surprisingly <u>observant</u>. 'Things weren't going well. The man who was holding the party was trying so hard, but it was no good. The tall, blonde woman on his right was as stiff as a <u>pole</u>, and the girl in the green dress on his left was desperate to sit next to the handsome, dark-haired man opposite. The fair man next to her looked ill and the black-haired woman next to him looked really nervous.'

'You seem to have noticed a great deal, Miss Shannon,' said Colonel Race.

'Well, actually, I wasn't having a very good time myself. I had gone out with this Mexican guy three nights in a row, and I was getting tired of him! He wanted to experience London night life, so we dined at the Compradour, and the Mille Fleurs, and then last night it was the Luxembourg. Champagne all the way – but his conversation was so boring! Just business deals he had done in Mexico, and all the women who were crazy about him. I got tired of listening after a while – so I just ate my supper and looked round the room.'

'Well, let's hope you saw something that may help us,' said Kemp.

Christine shook her head. 'I've no idea who killed the man. He just took a drink of champagne, went purple in the face and collapsed.'

'Do you remember when he had last drunk from his glass before that?'

She thought hard. 'Why, yes. After the cabaret, the lights went up, he picked up his glass and said something and the others picked up their glasses, too. They drank a toast of some kind. Then the music started and they all went off to dance, laughing for the first time. Champagne can do that for the dullest parties.'

'They left the table empty?'

'Yes.'

'And no one came near the table while they were away?'

'No one, except the waiter.'

'Which waiter?'

'One of the junior ones. Not the Italian.'

'And did this junior fill up the glasses?'

Christine shook her head. 'He just picked up an evening bag that one of the girls had dropped when they got up to dance, put it back on the table and went off again.'

'Whose bag was it?'

She concentrated. 'It was green and gold, so it belonged to the girl in the green dress. The other two had black bags.'

'Could someone else have gone to the table without you noticing?'

Christine shook her head. 'No. You see, Pedro had gone to make a telephone call, so I was just looking around. And there wasn't much to see, from where I was sitting, except the empty table next to us. Well, when they all came back to sit down, the man who died said something, and they all picked up their glasses again. And then it happened.' She paused. 'I thought it was a stroke. Pedro came back just then and I said, "Look, Pedro, that man's had a stroke." And he said, "He's passing out, that's all," which was pretty much what Pedro was doing himself. I had to keep my eye on him. They don't like you passing out at the Luxembourg.'

'That girl's an excellent witness,' Kemp said, as they left Miss Shannon's flat. 'If there had been anything to see, she would have seen it. It's a <u>conjuring trick</u>! George Barton drinks champagne, goes off to dance, comes back, drinks from the *same glass*, and suddenly it's full of cyanide! It's crazy!' He paused. 'That young waiter was the only person who was near the table while they were all away dancing.'

'If he had put anything in Barton's glass, Christine would have seen him,' Race remarked. 'I'm beginning to believe he did it himself. But if so, I'm sure he didn't know it was cyanide.'

'You mean someone gave it to him? Told him it was medicine of some kind?'

'Possibly.'

'Who? The Farradays?' asked Kemp.

'That's unlikely.'

'And Anthony Browne is equally unlikely, which leaves the loving sister-in-law …'

'And the loyal secretary.'

'Yes, she could have given him something like that.' Kemp looked at Race. 'I'm going to Kidderminster House now. What about you?'

'I'll go and see Miss Lessing,' said Race. 'I'll offer my sympathy. Maybe take her out to lunch.'

'So you think it's her, then?'

'I don't think anything – yet.'

Chapter 4

Chief Inspector Kemp arrived at Kidderminster house and the butler led him to the library, where Lord Kidderminster and the Farradays were waiting.

Lord Kidderminster shook his hand. 'Chief Inspector, we appreciate your kindness in coming here, instead of summoning my daughter and her husband to Scotland Yard. This is the second time that they have witnessed a violent death in the same restaurant, involving two members of the same family. Publicity of this kind can damage the reputation of a man in public life. The Commissioner of Police tells me that Barton's death is murder, not suicide. But *you* thought it was suicide, didn't you, Sandra, my dear?'

'It seemed so obvious,' she said, thoughtfully. 'We were at the same table where poor Rosemary poisoned herself last year. When we saw George Barton down in Sussex, during the summer, his behaviour was very strange. We thought he hadn't recovered from his wife's death. So, yes, suicide seemed possible. And I can't imagine why anyone would want to murder him.'

'Nor can I,' said Stephen. 'Barton was an excellent fellow. I don't think he had an enemy in the world.'

Chief Inspector Kemp paused for a moment before replying. 'What you say is quite correct, I'm sure. But before his death, George Barton told two people that he believed his wife had been poisoned by someone else. The party last night in honour of Miss Marle's birthday was actually supposed to reveal the identity of Rosemary Barton's killer. So, he was certainly not considering suicide.' Kemp's manner became slightly more official. 'Lady Alexandra, you said that Mr Barton's behaviour had been strange this summer. In what way?'

'Well, he was nervous. He couldn't concentrate on what was said to him.'

'Yes,' agreed Stephen. 'He looked ill, too. He had lost weight.'

'Did you notice any change in his attitude towards you and your husband? Was he less friendly, perhaps?'

'No, quite the opposite, in fact. He bought a country house near to ours.'

'Was Rosemary Barton a close friend of yours, Lady Alexandra?'

'No, we were not close.' She gave a light laugh. 'She was really Stephen's friend. She was interested in politics, and he enjoyed educating such a charming and attractive woman.'

And you're a very clever one, thought Kemp. *I wonder how much you really know about those two.* He continued aloud, 'What do you know about Anthony Browne, Lady Alexandra?'

'Nothing at all, but I have met him occasionally.'

Kemp turned to Stephen. 'Mr Farraday?'

'I probably know less than my wife does. She has danced with him, at least. He seems to be a pleasant chap.'

'Was he particularly close to Mrs Barton?'

Stephen frowned. 'They were friendly, that's all I can say.'

'And what can you tell me about Miss Lessing, Lady Alexandra?'

'She was Mr Barton's secretary. I've only met her twice – first on the evening that Mrs Barton died, and again last night.'

'Did you form the impression that she was in love with George Barton?'

'I have no idea.'

'Then, let us talk about the events of last night.'

The Farradays' evidence confirmed the important points about the tragic events. Barton had proposed a toast to Iris. They had drunk it and then got up to dance. George and Iris had returned first. When asked about the empty chair, they said that George was expecting a man called Colonel Race to join them later in the evening. When the lights were turned on again, after the cabaret, George had stared at the empty chair with a strange expression on his face, before proposing a toast to Iris's birthday.

Closing his notebook, Kemp rose to his feet. 'I'm grateful for your help.' He turned to Stephen. 'Mr Farraday, there are one or two other points where I think you could help me. Perhaps you could visit me at Scotland Yard, at a time that suits you? I know you're a busy man.'

The request was pleasant, but the message was serious. Somehow, Stephen managed a friendly smile. 'Certainly, Chief Inspector.'

CHAPTER 5

Ruth welcomed Colonel Race into her office with calm friendliness. She was smartly dressed, as always, but he noticed the dark circles under her eyes, and the sadness round her mouth.

'I'm glad you've come, Colonel. Mr Barton was expecting you to join us last night. I was surprised that he hadn't invited another woman to make an even number of guests...' She broke off. 'What do such details matter now? I feel so <u>stunned</u> this morning.'

'But you have still come into the office?'

'Of course.' She looked shocked. 'There is so much to arrange.'

'George told me how much he relied upon you,' said Race.

She swallowed hard and then said quietly, 'I was with him for nearly eight years, and I think he trusted me.'

'I'm sure of that,' Race went on. 'It is nearly lunch-time. Would you come and have lunch with me? I have a lot that I would like to say to you.'

'Thank you. I would like that very much.'

Race took Ruth to a quiet little restaurant, and they made polite, general conversation while they waited for their food. When the waiter had served them and left, she said, 'Do you want to talk about last night? I would like to talk about it, please. If I hadn't seen it happen, I wouldn't have believed it. Was it really murder, Colonel Race?'

'Did Kemp tell you that last night?'

'Not exactly, but it was clear what he was thinking.'

'Miss Lessing, you were with George for most of yesterday. Did he seem at all upset, or excited?'

66

She hesitated. 'It's difficult to say. He was upset, but there was a reason for that.' She told Race about Victor Drake, and his most recent demand for money.

'Hmm,' said Race. 'And Barton was upset about it?'

'He was annoyed, certainly, and he wanted to fix it quickly. It's happened before, several times, you see. In fact, last year Victor got into such trouble in this country that we had to send him to South America. But it seemed to me that he was actually angry because Victor's telegram arrived just as he was preparing his party at the Luxembourg, and he didn't want to think about anything else.'

'Did George tell you the real reason why he was having this party?'

She shook her head.

'He didn't tell you that he believed his wife had been murdered?'

She stared at him. 'George believed that?'

'Yes. He received two anonymous letters saying that his wife had been killed by someone else.'

'So *that's* why he was so strange this summer! And I knew nothing about it!' Ruth sounded upset. 'I see now that he must have had a plan in his head. Maybe he hoped that by recreating Rosemary's party again, he would find a clue of some kind. And that's why he didn't tell me about the letters! Because, if it was a murder, then one of us round the table must have killed her. It might even have been me!'

Race said, gently, 'Did you have any reason for killing Rosemary Barton?'

She looked down at the table and sighed. 'I think you had better know.' Then she met his eyes. 'I was in love with George. I was in love with him before he even met Rosemary. And I would have made him a good wife. I could have made him happy. He loved Rosemary, but he wasn't happy with her.'

'Did you dislike Rosemary?'

'Yes. I was shocked when she died, but I wasn't sorry. I was glad.' She paused. 'Please, can we talk about something else?'

'I'd like you to tell me, then, everything you can remember about yesterday.'

Ruth recalled George's anger over Victor's new demand for money, and the arrangements they made through their South American agent. Then she described arriving at the Luxembourg and continued her story up to the tragic moment. Her report confirmed the other accounts Race had already heard.

Ruth frowned. 'If it was murder, it couldn't have been done by any of us! So, who *did* put the poison into George's glass while we were dancing?'

'The evidence shows that no one else went near the table.'

'Then it doesn't make any sense!'

'Do you have *any* idea who might have put the cyanide in the glass? Was there anything at all suspicious, last night, however small?'

For a moment, she looked uncertain. Then she answered, 'Nothing.'

But there *had* been something. He was sure of that.

◆ ◆ ◆

After lunch, Ruth returned to the office, and Race drove to Elvaston Square.

Was it possible that Ruth Lessing was guilty, he wondered? She seemed honest and straightforward. But she certainly had a motive, at least for the first murder. With Rosemary gone, she had a good chance of becoming Mrs George Barton. Race thought that Ruth was too sensible to kill for money. But love? Perhaps. Loving George and hating Rosemary, she might well have coldly planned and executed Rosemary's death. The fact that a verdict of suicide had been passed could be just another example of her famous efficiency. But then George had received the anonymous letters and planned his trap. And so Ruth had silenced him... No, that didn't feel right. That suggested panic – and Ruth Lessing was not the type of woman who panicked. She was more intelligent than George and could easily avoid any trap that he might try to set.

So, it seemed that Ruth didn't fit after all...

CHAPTER 6

Lucilla Drake came into the sitting room, dressed in black, and held out a shaking hand to Colonel Race. She couldn't have seen anyone, she explained, except such an old friend of *dear* George's. It was dreadful to have no man in the house! She had no idea what to do. Of course Miss Lessing would manage all the business matters, and they must arrange the funeral – but what about the inquest?

Race said that she could depend on him for help. Lucilla was very grateful. Miss Lessing was very efficient, of course, but perhaps George had relied upon her too much. Of course Lucilla had known what the girl was planning, unlike dear Iris, who was such an innocent. And so quiet. It was impossible to know what she was thinking about. In fact, Lucilla had wanted Iris to see the doctor this summer, because she looked so pale and tired. 'But really, Colonel, I believe that was due to the location of the house. It was in a deep valley, you know, and there was always a damp mist around it in the evenings.' Poor George had bought it himself – such a pity. It would have been better if he had taken an older woman's advice. Men knew nothing about houses. She would have been happy to help – she had no other demands on her time, after all, with her husband dead for many years now, and her dear Victor away in Brazil.

Colonel Race said he had heard that she had a son abroad, and with that single encouragement, Lucilla told him all about her beloved Victor. He was such a handsome, clever boy, willing to <u>try his hand</u> at anything. Just look at all the different jobs he had done! And never unkind, or bad-tempered. 'But he's always been unlucky, Colonel. He was wrongly accused of a crime by the <u>headmaster</u> of his school. And then the authorities at Oxford University were so unfair. Of course an artistic boy would think it an excellent joke to copy someone else's handwriting. He did it for fun, not for money.'

Eventually Colonel Race managed to move Lucilla on from the subject of her son to that of servants. It was very difficult to find good servants these days, she agreed. They were lucky. Mrs Pound was an excellent cook, who had worked for them ever since George married. She had been happy to move to the country for the summer, unlike the parlourmaid[15], who had resigned. But that was for the best – she had no manners, and had also broken six of the best wine glasses. 'I mentioned it in her reference. For it is important to be truthful, Colonel Race, and faults must be noted as well as good qualities. But the girl was quite rude, and said that she hoped next time at least she wouldn't be working in the kind of house where people got murdered. Which was quite inaccurate, since poor Rosemary took her *own* life. And so, I wrote in her reference that the parlourmaid Betty Archdale was sober and honest, but that she broke things, and was not always polite to her employer. If I had been Mrs Rees-Talbot, I would not have employed her with such a reference. But people nowadays will take whatever they can get.'

Colonel Race asked if she meant the Mrs Rees-Talbot whose family he had known in India.

'I couldn't say. Cadogan Square was the address.'

'Those are my friends.'

Lucilla said that there were no friends like old friends. Friendship was a wonderful thing, wasn't it? She had always thought it was so romantic about Viola and Paul, for example. Dear Viola had been a lovely girl, with so many men in love with her... but, of course, Colonel Race wouldn't know who she was talking about. The Colonel asked to know the story. She happily told him about her brother Hector's marriage to the beautiful Viola, and how Paul Bennett had changed from lover into family friend, and godfather to Rosemary, to whom he had left his fortune on his death. 'And now dear Iris has inherited the money, and although I try to look out for fortune-hunters, one can't protect girls these days as one used to do. Iris has friends I know nothing about. Poor George was particularly worried about a man called Browne, and I always think that men are the best judges of other men.'

A faint sound made Race look round to see Iris Marle in the open doorway. 'Iris, dear!' cried Lucilla. 'Do you remember Colonel Race?'

Iris came in and shook hands. Race had met her once before, on his recent visit to Little Priors. Her black dress made her look thinner and paler than he remembered. She was clearly still suffering from shock.

'I came to see if I could be of any help to you,' said Race.

'Thank you. That was kind.' She turned to her aunt. 'Were you talking about Anthony just now?'

Lucilla blushed. 'Well, yes, as a matter of fact I did just mention that we know nothing about him...'

Iris interrupted her. 'You'll have every chance of doing so in future, because I'm going to marry him!'

'Oh, *Iris!*' Lucilla cried. 'You mustn't do anything foolish! Nothing can be decided at present. One can't talk about things like marriage when the funeral hasn't even taken place. It isn't fitting. The question simply doesn't come up.'

Iris laughed suddenly. 'But it has come up. Anthony asked me to marry him before we left Little Priors. He wanted me to come up to London and marry him the next day without telling anyone. I wish now that I had.'

'Wasn't that a rather strange request?' said Colonel Race, gently.

'No, it wasn't! And it would have saved a lot of trouble. He asked me to trust him and I didn't. But now I'll marry him as soon as he likes.'

Lucilla burst into tears.

'Miss Marle, might I speak to you privately before I leave?' asked Race. 'On a matter of business.'

'Why, yes,' she said, surprised, and walked to the door.

Race followed her across the hall, into a small room at the back of the house. 'All I wanted to say, Miss Marle,' he said, 'was that Chief Inspector Kemp is a friend of mine, and I'm sure you will find him both helpful and kind.'

She stared at him for a moment. 'Why didn't you come and join us last night, as George expected you to?'

'George didn't expect me.'

'He said he did.'

'He may have said so, but he knew I wasn't coming.'

'But that empty chair... Who was it for, then?' Her face went white. 'Rosemary...' she whispered. 'I see... It was for Rosemary.'

He thought she was going to faint. He caught hold of her, and helped her to sit down.

'I'm all right,' she said, out of breath. 'But I don't know what to do...'

'Can I help?'

She looked up at him unhappily. 'I must get things in order. George believed Rosemary was murdered, because of those letters. Colonel Race, who wrote those letters?'

'Nobody knows.'

'But George believed them, and arranged the party last night. There was an empty chair, and it was All Souls' Day. The Day of the Dead. A day when Rosemary's spirit could come back and – and tell him the truth.'

'You mustn't be too creative.'

'But George drank a toast to Rosemary – and then he died. Perhaps she came and took him.'

'The dead don't put cyanide in a champagne glass, my dear.'

His words seemed to steady her, and she said, in a more normal tone of voice, 'But it's incredible. The police think George was murdered, and I suppose it must be true. But it doesn't make sense.'

'No? If Rosemary was murdered, and George was beginning to suspect who—'

'But she *wasn't*! She had a reason for her suicide. I'll show you.'

She left the room and returned with Rosemary's letter in her hand, which she handed to him. 'Read for yourself.'

Race <u>unfolded</u> the paper and read it through.

'You see?' she said. 'Her heart was broken. She didn't want to go on living.'

'Do you know who that letter was written to?'

Iris nodded. 'Stephen Farraday. She was in love with him and he was cruel to her. So she took the cyanide to the restaurant and drank it there, where he could see her die. Perhaps she hoped he would be sorry then.'

'When did you find this?'

'About six months ago.'

'You didn't show it to George?'

'How *could* I betray my sister?' she cried, passionately. 'And George was so sure that she loved him. I couldn't tell him he was wrong. What do I do now? I've shown the letter to you because you were George's friend. Does Inspector Kemp need to see it?'

'Yes. It's evidence, you see. You should let me take it to him now.'

She gave a deep sigh. 'Very well.'

CHAPTER 7

Mary Rees-Talbot greeted Colonel Race with a cry of delight. 'My dear! I haven't seen you since you disappeared so mysteriously from Allahabad that time. Why are you here? You never make social visits. Come on, tell me the truth[16].'

Race smiled. 'Is Betty Archdale the maid who let me in?'

'Don't tell me she's a dangerous European spy!'

'No, no. She's just a parlourmaid. But I think she may be able to tell me something.'

'I'm sure you're right. She's the kind of servant who always manages to be passing by when there's anything interesting going on. What do you want me to do?'

'Offer me a drink, then call for Betty and order it.'

'And when Betty brings it?'

'Then please go away.'

'Oh, all right, then. I'll play!'

Mrs Rees-Talbot rang the bell for Betty and asked her to bring Colonel Race a whisky and <u>soda</u>. When Betty returned with the drink on a tray, Mrs Rees-Talbot was standing by the door.

'Colonel Race has some questions to ask you,' she said, and went out.

Betty looked at the tall, grey-haired soldier with alarm. He took the glass from the tray and smiled. 'Have you seen the papers today?' he asked.

'Yes, sir,' she said, cautiously.

'Did you read that Mr George Barton died last night at the Luxembourg Restaurant?'

'Oh, yes, sir.' Betty's eyes <u>sparkled</u> with pleasure at the chance to discuss the public scandal. 'Wasn't it dreadful?'

'You were in service with the Bartons, weren't you?'

'Yes, sir. I left soon after Mrs Barton died. Was Mr Barton murdered, too? The papers didn't say exactly.'

'Why do you say "too", Betty? Mrs Barton's death was judged to be a suicide.'

She glanced at him doubtfully. 'Yes, sir.'

'Didn't you think it was?'

'No, sir. Not really.'

'Why not?'

'Well,' Betty hesitated. 'It was something I heard one day.'

'Yes?' he encouraged her.

'Well, I would never go and listen at a door, or anything, but I was going through the hall carrying a tray, and the parlour door wasn't shut, and Mrs Barton and Mr Browne were speaking quite loudly. She said something about Anthony Browne not being his name. And Mr Browne threatened to cut her face. Then he said if she didn't do what he told her, he would murder her! I didn't hear any more, because Miss Iris was coming down the stairs. I didn't think much of it at the time, but after Mrs Barton committed suicide at that party, and I heard Mr Browne had been there at the time – well, it scared me!'

'But you didn't say anything?'

She shook her head. 'I didn't want to get mixed up with the police. And perhaps if I had said anything, I would have been murdered, too! And, anyway, it might have been a joke. Mr Browne was always joking, so I couldn't tell, sir, could I?'

Race agreed that she couldn't. 'Mrs Barton said Browne wasn't his real name. Did she mention his real name?'

'Yes, and he said "Forget about Tony"… Tony something… Reminded me of the cherry jam that Cook had been making.'

'Tony Cheriton? Cherable?'

She shook her head again. 'It began with an M. It sounded foreign.'

'Well, if you remember, write to me at the address on this card.' Race handed Betty his business card and a pound note.

'I will, sir. Thank you, sir.'

As she left the room, Mary Rees-Talbot returned. 'Well, was it successful?'

'Yes. There's just one problem. Maybe you can help me. Can you think of a name that would remind you of cherry jam?'

'What an extraordinary question!'

'Please, Mary.'

'Well, we don't often make cherry jam. It's much too sweet, unless you use cooking cherries. Morello cherries.'

'That's it!' Race exclaimed. 'Mary, I'm very grateful. Could you ring that bell again, so that Betty comes to show me out?'

'Aren't you going to tell me what it's all about?' she asked, indignantly.

'I promise to come back and tell you the whole story,' he called as he left the room.

Betty was waiting in the hall with his hat and coat. He thanked her and walked out of the front door. At the top of the steps, he paused. 'By the way, Betty,' he said, 'was the name Morelli?'

Betty smiled. 'Quite right, sir! Tony Morelli!'

CHAPTER 8

At Scotland Yard, Chief Inspector Kemp was interviewing Pierre, one of six junior waiters at the Luxembourg, and having to accept that Pierre had done no more than pick up a lady's bag from the floor and put it back beside her plate.

'I am hurrying past with a sauce, when the young lady knocks her bag from the table as she goes to dance, so I pick it up and put it back, and then I hurry on. That is all, Monsieur.'

Kemp dismissed him, and was sitting at his desk, disappointed, when Sergeant Pollock arrived to report that a Miss Chloe West was asking for the officer in charge of the Luxembourg case.

'Very well, bring her in,' said Kemp.

Chloe West was twenty-five, tall, brown-haired and very pretty. She looked familiar to Kemp, although he was sure that he had never met her before.

'What can I do for you, Miss West?' he asked.

'I read in the paper about the man who died at the Luxembourg.'

'George Barton? Did you know him?'

'Not exactly.'

'Can I have your full name and address, please?'

'Chloe Elizabeth West. 15 Merryvale Court, Maida Vale. I'm an actress.'

'Yes?'

'Well, when I read that the police were inquiring into Mr Barton's death, I thought I should come and tell you something. It may not be anything to do with it, but...'

'I'll be the judge of that,' said Kemp pleasantly. 'Go on.'

'Well, Mr Barton saw my photograph in *Spotlight*, which is the actors' professional <u>directory</u>. He contacted me and said he had a job for me. He was having a dinner party at the Luxembourg and he wanted to surprise his guests. I met him and he showed me a photograph and told me that he wanted me to dress up as the person in the picture. I looked very similar, he said.'

Of course! That was why she was familiar! Chloe West looked like the photograph of Rosemary that Kemp had seen on the desk in George's study.

'He gave me the dress he wanted me to wear – it's a grey-green silk. He asked me to change my hair to the colour in the photograph, and copy the make-up. Then I was supposed to come into the Luxembourg restaurant during the cabaret show and sit down in the empty seat at Mr Barton's table.'

'Why didn't you keep the appointment, Miss West?'

'Because at about eight o'clock that night, someone telephoned me to say that the party had been cancelled. Then, the next morning, I read about the death in the papers.'

'And very sensibly you came along to us,' said Kemp. 'Thank you very much, Miss West. You've explained the mystery of the empty chair. By the way, was the person who telephoned you a man?'

'I'm not sure. I think so. But it sounded as though he had a cold.'

When Chloe West had gone, Kemp said to Sergeant Pollock, 'So *that* was George Barton's plan. And that's why he sat looking at that empty chair after the cabaret. His clever plan had gone wrong.'

'You don't think it was him who cancelled the job?'

'No. In fact, it may not have been a man at all. A cold can change your voice. We're making progress at last!'

CHAPTER 9

Stephen Farraday arrived at Scotland Yard later that same day, feeling very nervous. Why had Chief Inspector Kemp asked him for this extra interview? What did he suspect?

Kemp greeted him pleasantly enough, and invited him to sit down. Stephen noticed a police officer sitting at a table in the corner of the room with a pencil and a notebook.

'I wish to take a statement from you, Mr Farraday. That statement will be written down and you will be asked to read it and sign it before you leave. However, it is my duty to tell you that you may refuse to make such a statement and that you are also allowed to have a lawyer present if you wish.'

'That sounds very serious, Chief Inspector. But why do you need another statement from me? You heard all I had to say this morning.'

'There are certain facts, Mr Farraday, which I thought you would prefer to discuss here. Anything that is not relevant to a case we try to keep private. I'm sure you understand what I am referring to.'

'I'm afraid not.'

Kemp sighed. 'You had a 'close relationship' with the late Mrs Rosemary Barton…'

'Who says so?' Stephen interrupted.

Kemp picked up a letter from his desk. 'This letter was found amongst the late Mrs Barton's belongings. It was handed to us by Miss Iris Marle, who confirms it is her sister's handwriting.'

Stephen read the letter and a wave of sickness passed over him. He could hear Rosemary's voice, begging him… Would the past never die? He looked up at Kemp. 'There is no proof that this letter was written to me.'

'Do you pay the rent for 21 Malland Mansions, Earl's Court?'

So, they had found the flat he had rented, where he and Rosemary used to meet. They knew everything! Stephen shrugged his shoulders. 'May I ask why my private affairs should be of interest to you?'

'They are not, unless they are connected to the death of George Barton.'

'So you are suggesting that I had an affair with his wife, and then murdered him?'

'Mr Farraday, let's be honest. You and Mrs Barton were very close friends. *You* ended the relationship, not the lady. She intended to make trouble. And then, very conveniently, she died.'

'She committed *suicide.*'

'George Barton didn't think so. He started to ask questions – and then he died. There is a pattern to it.'

'Why are you accusing me?'

'Mrs Barton's death was lucky for you, wasn't it? A scandal would have ruined your political career. Did your wife know about the affair, Mr Farraday?'

'Certainly not. And I hope she will never learn about it now.'

'Is your wife a jealous woman?'

'No. She is much too sensible.'

'Do you keep a supply of cyanide at your country house, Mr Farraday?'

'I believe the gardener may have some.'

'But you have never purchased any yourself?'

'I have never purchased cyanide.'

Kemp asked Farraday a few more questions, then let him go.

'He was very quick to deny that his wife knew about his affair,' he said thoughtfully to his colleague. 'You would think he would realize that if his wife didn't know about the affair, that gave him an extra motive for silencing Rosemary Barton. The clever story would be to say that his wife knew about the affair and had accepted it.'

At that moment, the telephone rang. It was Colonel Race, calling from a public telephone box. Their conversation was short, but satisfactory.

'I'll send a telegram to America at once,' Kemp announced. 'We should hear back almost immediately. It will be a great relief if you are right.'

'I think I am,' said Colonel Race.

CHAPTER 10

Anthony Browne frowned at the card the hotel porter was holding out to him. Then he shrugged his shoulders. 'All right, show him up.'

He was standing at his window when the tall, military-looking man came in. A man he knew a great deal about. 'Colonel Race?' he said pleasantly. 'You were a friend of George Barton's, I know.' He offered him a chair. 'A cigarette?'

'Thank you.'

Anthony lit a match for him. 'You were the guest who didn't arrive that night – lucky for you.'

'You're wrong. That empty chair wasn't for me.'

Anthony was surprised. 'Really? Barton said…'

'He may have said so, but his plan was quite different. That chair was meant to be occupied, while the lights were off, by a girl called Chloe West, a young actress who looks like Rosemary Barton.'

Anthony whistled. 'I see.'

'She had been given a photograph of Rosemary and asked to copy her appearance. She even had the dress which Rosemary wore the night she died.' Race continued.

'Then the lights go on, and as people cry in fear and horror, they see Rosemary back from the dead. And the guilty person cries out, "I did it!"' Browne did not believe it. 'What a terrible idea. A real killer isn't going to behave like a silly schoolgirl. If somebody poisoned Rosemary Barton, and was about to do the same to George, they had a lot of confidence, and it would take more than an actress in <u>fancy dress</u> to make them confess.'

'Ah, but remember that in Shakespeare's play, Macbeth panicked when he saw the ghost of Banquo[17] he had killed. So, how about that, Mr Tony Morelli?'

There was a silence. Anthony sat down, and threw his cigarette into the fire. 'How did you find out?'

'You admit that you are Tony Morelli?'

'Why deny it? I expect you've got my details from America.'

'And you admit that when Rosemary Barton discovered your real identity, you threatened to murder her unless she kept quiet?'

'I tried to frighten her,' agreed Tony, pleasantly.

Colonel Race stared uncertainly at the man sitting opposite him. 'Shall I tell you exactly what we know about you, Morelli?'

'It might be amusing.'

'You were <u>convicted</u> in the United States of trying to sabotage the Ericsen aeroplane works and were sent to prison. At the end of your sentence, you vanished. You were next discovered in London staying at Claridge's and calling yourself Anthony Browne. There you met Lord Dewsbury, and other important armaments manufacturers. You stayed with Lord Dewsbury, and he chose to share some top-secret information with you. It is a strange coincidence, Morelli, that a trail of mysterious accidents and some lucky escapes from industrial disasters occurred soon after your visits to various important armaments factories.'

'Coincidences,' said Anthony, 'are extraordinary things.'

'You returned to London and <u>befriended</u> Iris Marle, making excuses not to visit her home, so that her family would not realize how close you were becoming. Finally you tried to persuade her to marry you in secret.'

'And why not? I've served my prison sentence. I've made some useful friends. I've fallen in love with a charming girl and I'm keen to marry her.'

'So keen that you wanted the wedding to happen before her family could discover your background. Iris Marle is a very rich young woman.'

Anthony nodded. 'Families can be horribly interfering. Iris doesn't know anything about my criminal past. And I would rather she didn't.'

'I'm afraid she is going to learn all about it. Perhaps you don't realize—'

Anthony laughed. 'Oh, I know what you're thinking. Rosemary Barton found out about me, so I killed her. George suspected me, so I killed him! And now I'm after Iris's money! It all makes sense, but you can't prove a thing!'

Race watched him carefully for some minutes. Then he got up from his chair. 'All the facts about your past are true,' he said. 'And it's all wrong.'

Anthony narrowed his eyes. 'What's wrong?'

'You are. The story made sense until I saw you, but now it won't work. You're not a criminal. You're one of us, aren't you? A British Agent?'

Anthony smiled slowly. 'Yes. That's why I've tried to avoid meeting you. I was afraid that you would guess what I am, and it was important that nobody knew – until yesterday. Now, thank goodness, it's all over. We've caught the gang of international criminals we've been hunting for the last three years. I've been working <u>undercover</u>, going to meetings, making connections inside the gang. At last, my chief decided that I had to commit a real crime and go to prison. It was the most certain way to convince the gang I was one of them.

'When I came out of prison, they trusted me, and I gradually worked my way towards the centre of the operation. It was an international network, run from Central Europe. Acting as the gang's agent I came to London and stayed at Claridge's hotel. They had ordered me to make friends with Lord Dewsbury, so I joined the London social scene, and that's how I met Rosemary Barton.

'But one day I was shocked to learn that she knew I had been in prison in America as Tony Morelli. I was terrified for her safety! The criminals I was working for would have killed her immediately if they thought she knew about me. I tried to frighten her into keeping her mouth shut, but I couldn't trust her to keep quiet.

'So, I decided to leave London – and then I saw Iris coming down the stairs. I promised myself that once my <u>mission</u> was finished, I would come back and marry her. When my part in the operation was over, I returned to London and found her again. I stayed away from her family, because I knew they would make inquiries about my background and I needed to stay undercover for a bit longer. But I began to worry about her. She looked ill and afraid – and George Barton was behaving very strangely. I asked her to come away and marry me, but she refused.

'And then I was invited to this party. As we sat down to dinner, George said you would be coming, so I told him that I had met a man I knew and might have to leave early. Actually I *had* seen someone I knew in America – Monkey Coleman – and I wanted to avoid him. But I really wanted to escape meeting you, as I was still undercover. And then George died. I had nothing to do with his death, or Rosemary's. I still don't know who did kill them.'

'Any idea?'

'It must have been either the waiter or one of the people at the table. I don't think it was the waiter. It wasn't me or Iris. It could have been one, or both, of the Farradays. Ruth Lessing seems to me to be the most likely person. But on both nights she was sitting in a place from which it was impossible for her to poison the champagne glass.' Anthony paused. 'Have you found out who wrote those anonymous letters yet?'

Race shook his head. 'No. I thought I had – but I was wrong.'

'Because someone knows that Rosemary was murdered. And, unless you're careful, that person will be murdered next!'

Chapter 11

On the day of the inquest into George's death, Anthony arrived at Elvaston Square at half-past five in the afternoon. He was told by the new parlourmaid that Iris had just come in, and was in the study.

Iris jumped nervously as he entered the room. 'Oh, it's you,' she said.

Anthony came quickly towards her. 'What's the matter, darling?'

'Nothing.' She paused. 'Only – I was nearly run over. Oh, it was my own fault. I was thinking so hard, I crossed the road without looking, and a car came round a corner really fast and just missed me.'

Anthony held her gently. 'Oh, Iris, I'm worried about you – not about your incredible escape from under the wheels of a car, but about why you're wandering about in the middle of the road. What's worrying you, my darling?'

'I'm afraid,' she said, quietly.

Anthony sat down beside her on a sofa. 'Come on.' He smiled, encouragingly. 'Tell me all about it.'

'I don't know if you'll believe me. It's about… the other night. You were at the inquest this morning, so you heard…' She broke off, her eyes wide and dark with fear.

'Very little,' said Anthony. 'The police doctor talked about the effects of cyanide. The police inspector, who was the first to arrive at the Luxembourg, gave his report. George's body was identified by his chief clerk. And then the inquest was closed for a week.'

'That police inspector described finding a small paper sachet under the table, containing signs of cyanide.'

'Yes. Well, clearly whoever put the poison into George's glass then dropped the container under the table. Couldn't risk having it found on him – or her.'

Iris began to shake. 'No, Anthony. *I* dropped that packet under the table!'

He stared at her in amazement.

'You remember how George drank that champagne and then it happened?' she said.

He nodded.

'It was like some horrible dream. After the cabaret, when the lights went on again, I was so happy. Because that was the moment when we found Rosemary dead before, and I was so afraid that I would see it all again... see her lying dead across the table. But there was nothing there, and suddenly it felt as if the whole thing really was over at last, and everything would be all right again. So I danced with George, and started to enjoy myself at last.

'Then we came back to the table, and George asked us to drink to Rosemary's memory, and then he died and the nightmare was back again. I just stood there, shaking. And suddenly I started to cry. I opened my bag to get my handkerchief, and I found something <u>tangled up</u> inside it. It was a paper sachet, the kind you get medicine powders in from the chemist. But it wasn't in my bag when I left home! I had packed a powder <u>compact</u>, a <u>lipstick</u>, a handkerchief, a comb, and some loose coins. So, someone else must have put that sachet in my bag. And I remembered how they had found a sachet like that in Rosemary's bag after *she* died, with cyanide in it, so I dropped it under the table. I was really frightened. Somebody meant it to look as though *I* killed George, and I *didn't*.'

Anthony whistled. 'Did anyone see you do it?'

Iris hesitated. 'I think Ruth may have. But she was so shocked that I don't know if she actually noticed – or if she was just staring through me.'

'Why weren't your fingerprints on it, I wonder?'

'I was holding it through the handkerchief.'

Anthony nodded. 'That was lucky.'

'But who could have put it in my bag? I had it beside me all the evening.'

'No. When you went to dance after the cabaret, you left it on the table. Somebody could have done it then – or when you visited the ladies' cloakroom as you arrived. Can you remember what happened in there?

Iris thought. 'We all went to the long table, put our bags down and checked our make-up in the mirrors. Ruth put powder on her nose, and Sandra tidied up her hair. I gave my coat to the <u>attendant</u>, and went over to the sinks.'

'Leaving your bag on the table?'

'Yes. I washed my hands, while Ruth finished her make-up and Sandra gave her coat to the attendant. Then Sandra returned to the mirror, Ruth came over to wash her hands and I went back to the table to comb my hair.'

'So, either of them could have put something in your bag without you seeing?'

'Yes, but I can't believe they would do such a thing. And if it was Ruth, why didn't she say she saw me drop the packet?'

'I don't know. So it looks as though it wasn't her…'

Iris sighed. 'I'm so glad I've told you. No one else needs to know, do they?'

Anthony looked embarrassed. 'I'm afraid they do, Iris. In fact you're going to come with me now in a taxi, to tell Kemp.'

'Oh, no, Anthony! They'll think I killed George.'

'They're more likely to think so if they find out later that you kept quiet about this!'

'*Please,* Anthony.'

'Look here, Iris, you're in a difficult position. But you must tell the truth. You can't play safe when it's a question of justice. Come on, we're going to see Kemp! Now!'

As she followed him unwillingly into the hall, the front door bell rang.

'Oh, I forgot!' exclaimed Iris. 'Ruth said she would come over after work to discuss the funeral arrangements. Aunt Lucilla has gone to have tea with a friend, and I thought we could organize things better while she was out. She does confuse things so.'

Anthony stepped forward and opened the door. Ruth was looking tired and carrying a large briefcase. 'I'm sorry I'm late. The train was terribly crowded tonight and then I had to wait for three buses. There wasn't a taxi anywhere.'

Iris said, 'I can't come now, Anthony.'

'You must.' said Anthony. 'I'm sorry to take Iris away, Miss Lessing, but it can't be avoided.'

'That's all right, Mr Browne. I'll fix everything with Mrs Drake when she comes back.'

'Come on,' said Anthony, and pulled Iris out through the open door.

A taxi was approaching along the square. Anthony stopped it and asked the driver to take them to Scotland Yard.

CHAPTER 12

An hour or two later, three men were sitting at a small round table in a café. Colonel Race and Chief Inspector Kemp were drinking cups of dark brown tea. Anthony was drinking the café's idea of a nice cup of coffee. It was certainly not Anthony's idea.

Chief Inspector Kemp, having checked into Anthony's real background carefully, had decided to accept him as a colleague. 'If you ask me,' he said, putting sugar into his tea and stirring it, 'this case will never <u>come to trial</u>. Our only hope was to find evidence of the purchasing or handling of cyanide by one of those five suspects, but we haven't. It'll be one of those cases where you know who did it, but simply can't prove it.'

'Do you know who did it?' asked Anthony.

'Oh, I'm pretty certain it was Lady Alexandra Farraday. I believe she's the jealous type. I doubt Mr Barton would have bought that house in the country unless he suspected one of the Farradays. He must have made it pretty obvious, insisting that they come to his party, so she decided to <u>finish him off</u>! That's just theory, but the fact is that the only person who could have dropped something into Mr Barton's glass just before he drank, would be Lady Alexandra, who was sitting on his right.'

'Just one point,' interrupted Race. 'Even if Lady Alexandra is a jealous woman, capable of murder, could she slip <u>incriminating</u> evidence into an innocent girl's handbag? A girl who has never done her any harm? Could the daughter of the Kidderminsters do such a thing?'

Inspector Kemp stared unhappily into his teacup for a moment, then decided to change the subject. 'Mr Browne,' he said, turning to Anthony, 'and I'll still call you that, if you don't mind – I want to thank you for bringing Miss Marle straight to me this evening to tell her story.'

'She didn't want to come, I imagine?' said Colonel Race.

'She's terrified, poor girl,' said Anthony.

'Naturally,' said the Chief Inspector, 'but I think we reassured her. She went home quite happy.'

'You may be right, Chief Inspector, that the case will never come to trial – but that's a very unsatisfactory ending. And we still don't know who wrote those letters to George!'

'Are your suspicions still the same, Browne?' asked Race.

'Yes, Ruth Lessing is my bet for the murderer. She was in love with George, and I believe Rosemary treated her pretty badly. I think she saw a chance to get rid of Rosemary, and then marry George herself.'

'Ruth Lessing has the cool character that could plan and carry out a murder, and she certainly has the motive for the first killing,' agreed Race. 'But why would she then poison the man she loved and wanted to marry! And if she had hidden the cyanide packet in Iris's bag, why did she keep quiet about seeing her throw it under the table?'

'Perhaps she didn't see it,' suggested Anthony, doubtfully.

'I think she did. When I interviewed her, I knew she was hiding something.'

'So, who gets your vote, Colonel?' asked Kemp.

Race looked at the other men thoughtfully. 'You have both chosen female suspects. And I also suspect a woman.' He paused. 'I think the guilty person is Iris Marle.'

Anthony pushed his chair back with a crash, his face red with anger. With an effort, he controlled himself, and although his voice shook slightly, it sounded as light and mocking as ever. 'By all means let us discuss the idea. Why Iris? And if so, why should she tell me about dropping the cyanide paper under the table?'

'Because she knew that Ruth had seen her do it.'

Anthony nodded. 'Very well. So, why do you suspect her?'

'The motive,' said Race. 'Rosemary inherited an enormous fortune, in which Iris had no share, but if Rosemary died childless, the money would be hers. Rosemary was depressed, exhausted by her illness, in just the mood where a verdict of suicide would be accepted.'

'And then George showed her those anonymous letters, and she panicked and murdered him, too? Is that what you think?'

'Yes.'

'So, how did she get the cyanide into George's glass?'

'I don't know.'

'Well, I'm glad there's something you don't know.' Anthony's eyes were dangerous. 'Right, then,' he continued, rapidly, 'things have changed and we simply have to solve this case now. I'll state the questions again. Who knew that Rosemary had been murdered? And who wrote to George telling him so? Well, I'm afraid we'll have to ignore that first murder for now. It's too long ago, and we don't know exactly what happened. But I saw the second murder take place, so I should know how it happened.

'The perfect time to put the cyanide in George's glass was during the cabaret, but it couldn't have been done then because he drank from the glass straight afterwards. Nobody else touched his glass, but the next time he drank from it, it was full of cyanide. He couldn't have been poisoned – but he was! It was a conjuring trick... *Oh, of course!*' He held his head in his hands, in obvious mental distress. 'That's it... *that's it*... for lots and lots of money – and maybe love as well? The bag... the waiter... *Yes!*'

He dropped his hands and stared at the other two men. 'Don't you see? A waiter could have poisoned the champagne, but not *the* waiter who was serving them! And *George* and George's *glass* are *two different things!* Come on, I'll show you.' He jumped to his feet.

Kemp looked at his half-full teacup with regret. 'I have to pay the bill,' he muttered.

'No, no, we'll be back in a moment. I must show you outside. Come on.'

Pushing their chairs out of the way, he hurried the others into the entrance hall of the café. 'Do you see that telephone box over there?'

'Yes?'

Anthony felt in his pockets. 'Oh no, I haven't got a coin for the call. Never mind. I'd rather not do that, actually. Let's go back.'

They returned to the table. Kemp picked up his pipe and began to clean it out.

Race looked at Anthony, puzzled, and picked up his cup to finish his tea. 'Goodness me,' he said in great surprise. 'It's got sugar in it!' He looked across at Anthony, who smiled at him.

'And what on earth is this?' said Kemp, after tasting his own cup.

'Coffee,' said Anthony. 'I don't think you'll like it. I didn't.'

CHAPTER 13

As Anthony watched understanding appear in the eyes of the other men, a new thought hit him. 'Just a minute – that *car!*' he cried, and jumped to his feet. 'I'm a fool! An idiot! Iris told me that a car had nearly run her over – and I hardly listened. Come on, quick!'

'She said she was going straight home when she left Scotland Yard,' said Kemp.

'Who's at the house?' asked Race.

'Ruth Lessing was there, waiting for Mrs Drake to come home and discuss the funeral.'

'Discussing everything else as well, if I know Mrs Drake,' said Race. He added quickly, 'Has Iris Marle got any other relations?'

'Not that I know of.'

'I see the direction in which your thoughts are leading you. But – is it physically possible?'

'I think so. Consider for yourself how much has been taken for granted *on one person's word.*'

'You think that Miss Marle is in danger?' asked Kemp as he paid the bill.

'Yes, I do.'

The three men hurried out of the café and stopped a taxi, telling the driver to go to Elvaston Square as quickly as possible.

'I've only got the general idea so far,' said Kemp, as they raced through the London streets. 'It certainly clears the Farradays, thank goodness. But surely there wouldn't be another murder so soon?'

'The sooner the better,' said Race. 'Before anyone realizes the truth. Iris told me, in front of Mrs Drake, that she would marry Browne as soon as he wanted her to.'

As the taxi drew up in Elvaston Square, Anthony jumped out and ran up the steps to ring the bell, while Race paid the fare. Kemp followed Anthony up the steps as the parlourmaid opened the door.

'Is Miss Iris back?' asked Anthony, anxiously.

'Yes, sir. Half an hour ago.'

He sighed with relief. 'Where is she?'

'I expect she's in the sitting room with Mrs Drake.'

Anthony nodded and went up the stairs to the sitting room, Race and Kemp following behind him.

In the sitting room, they found Lucilla Drake searching for a letter in her desk.

'Where's Iris?' demanded Anthony.

Lucilla stared at him. 'I beg your pardon? Who are you?' Recognizing Race, she smiled. She did not notice Chief Inspector Kemp also entering the room. 'Colonel Race! How kind of you to come! But I do wish you could have been here a little earlier – I would have liked to ask you about the funeral arrangements. I was so upset that I couldn't really think. Miss Lessing was very kind, and offered to do everything she could to help me. But, naturally I am the person most likely to know what George's favourite <u>hymns</u> were – not that he went to church very often...'

As she paused to take a breath, Race asked, 'Where is Miss Marle?'

'She said she had a headache and was going up to her room. I said that was quite all right. Miss Lessing and I were managing perfectly well, and she could leave everything to us.'

'Has Miss Lessing gone?' asked Kemp.

'Yes, she went about ten minutes ago. <u>Canon</u> Westbury is to give the funeral service...'

As Lucilla went on talking, Anthony backed silently out of the door and ran up the stairs. Chief Inspector Kemp followed close behind him. They were on the second floor landing, when Anthony heard a light <u>footstep</u> coming down the stairs from the floor above. He pulled Kemp behind a nearby bathroom door.

As the footsteps continued down the stairs, Anthony came out of the bathroom and ran up to the third floor. Iris's room, he knew, was at the back of the house. He knocked on the door. 'Iris!' There was no reply. He tried the handle. The door was locked. In sudden fear, he beat loudly upon it. 'Iris – *Iris!*' Looking down, he saw that a <u>mat</u> had been pushed up against the bottom of the door. He kicked it away and lay down to press his nose against the gap. He smelt the air, then jumped up and shouted *'Kemp!'*

There was no reply from the Chief Inspector, but Colonel Race came running up the stairs.

'Gas, pouring out!' cried Anthony. 'We'll have to break the door down.'

The two men ran at the door. The lock broke, and the door flew open.

'She's by the fire,' said Race. 'I'll break the window. You get her out.'

Iris was lying, unconscious, by the gas fire, her face beside the open gas tap. Coughing and <u>choking</u> from the smoke, Anthony carried her out onto the stairs and laid her on the floor.

'I'll look after her,' said Race. 'Go and call a doctor. Don't worry. She'll be all right. We got here just in time.'

CHAPTER 14

Iris was lying on a sofa, in the sitting room at Little Priors, where she had been taken to recover from her terrible experience. 'And now, please, Tony, will you tell me all about it?' she asked.

Anthony smiled widely at Colonel Race, who was sitting by the window in the morning sunshine. 'I must say, I've been looking forward to this moment. If I don't tell people how clever I've been, I shall burst. So, here goes.

'George discovered that Rosemary's death wasn't suicide after all, and he started to investigate, but before he could reveal her killer, he was also murdered. However, his murder was impossible. George couldn't be poisoned, but George was poisoned. Nobody touched George's glass, but George's glass was <u>tampered with</u>.

'And then I realized the one important point. George's ear is George's ear, because it is fixed to his head and cannot be removed without an operation! But George's watch might belong to him, or might have been lent to him by someone else. In the same way, 'George's wine glass' simply means the glass from which he has just been drinking. There is nothing else to separate it from several other similar glasses.

'To prove this, I made an experiment. Race was drinking tea without sugar, Kemp was drinking tea with sugar, and I was drinking coffee. All three drinks looked similar. We were sitting at one of several small, round tables in a café. I made an excuse and hurried the others out into the entrance hall, knocking their chairs out of position as we stood up. I also secretly moved Kemp's pipe, which was lying beside his cup, to the same position beside *my* cup.

'When we returned, Kemp pulled his chair up to the table again, and sat beside his pipe. Race sat on his right, and I sat on his left, as before. But now, the impossible had happened. Before, Kemp's cup had sweet tea in it. Now Kemp's cup contained coffee. These two facts can't both be true – but they are. Because Kemp's cup when he left the table, and Kemp's cup when he returned, are not the same thing.

'And that is what happened at the Luxembourg that night, Iris. After the cabaret, when you went to dance, you dropped your bag. A waiter picked it up – not the waiter who was serving your table and knew which seat was yours, but *another* waiter who was hurrying past and quickly picked up the bag and put it beside the plate one place to the left of yours. When you returned, you went to the place marked by your bag, and George sat down on your right. When he proposed his toast in memory of Rosemary, he drank from *what he thought* was *his* glass but was actually *your* glass. A glass which could have been poisoned earlier, because the only person who did not drink straight after the cabaret, was the person who was being toasted by the other guests – and that means *you,* Iris! *You* were the intended victim, not George! If things had gone as planned, we would have seen the suicide of the second Marle sister. A piece of paper which had contained cyanide is found in her bag, and the case is clear! The poor girl could not cope with her sister's death.'

Iris interrupted him. 'But why should anyone want to kill *me*?'

'Money, my darling! You inherited Rosemary's fortune. But if you died without marrying, the money would then go to your closest relative – your Aunt Lucilla. And then who else would benefit? Victor Drake, who has always exploited his unfortunate mother. It's easy to see Victor as a killer. And from the very start of the case, he has been hiding in the shadows.'

'But Victor has been in South America for over a year!'

'Has he really? You see, this story starts with "Girl meets Boy!" When Ruth Lessing met Victor, I think she fell in love with him. Those quiet, sensible women often fall for bad men. And the evidence that Victor was in South America depends entirely on Ruth's word. It was Ruth who reported that Victor had sailed away on the *S.S. Cristobal* before Rosemary's death! And it was Ruth who suggested telephoning Buenos Aires on the day of George's death, then dismissed the telephone operator who knew she did not make the call.

'In fact, Victor Drake had left Buenos Aires several weeks before, but he left behind a telegram to be sent in his name on a certain date – another demand for money – which would prove that he was still there. Instead of which, he was the Mexican sitting with a girlfriend at the table next to ours at the Luxembourg! Bad skin and <u>bloodshot</u> eyes make a simple but effective disguise. In our party, I was the only person apart from Ruth Lessing who had ever seen Victor Drake, but I was sitting with my back to him. As we came into the restaurant, I did recognize a man I wanted to avoid, who I had known in prison as Monkey Coleman. But I never imagined that he was connected to the crime, or that he and Victor Drake were the same man.'

'But how did he do it?'

'It was simple,' said Colonel Race. 'During the cabaret he went out to make a telephone call, passing our table on the way. In the past, Drake had been both an actor and a waiter. Pedro Morales was an easy role for an actor to play, but to move professionally around a table, filling up champagne glasses, required the skill of a man who had actually been a waiter. And none of you noticed him. You were watching the cabaret, not the waiter.'

'And it was Ruth who put the cyanide paper in your bag,' said Anthony. 'Probably in the cloakroom when you first arrived. She did the same thing to Rosemary, a year ago.'

'I always thought it strange that George hadn't told Ruth about those letters. He took her advice about everything.'

Anthony laughed. 'Of course he told her. She knew he would. That's why she wrote them. Then she helped him to arrange his plan, and so she prepared nicely for suicide number two – which would be yours.'

'And to think I actually wanted her to marry George!'

'She would probably have made him a very good wife, if she hadn't met Victor.'

Iris shivered. 'Just for money!'

'Victor certainly did it for money. Ruth did it for money, for Victor, and also, I think, because she hated Rosemary. She had changed greatly by the time she tried to run you down in a car, and still further when she left Lucilla in the sitting room, and ran up to your bedroom. Did she seem dangerous when you saw her?'

Iris considered. 'No. She just knocked on my door, came in and said everything was arranged and she hoped I was feeling all right. I said I was quite tired. And after that I don't remember anything.'

'Because she hit you on the head and knocked you unconscious, darling. Then she put you by the gas fire, turned on the tap and went out, locking the door and sliding the key back underneath it. She pushed the mat up against the door to <u>seal</u> it, and went quietly back down the stairs. Kemp and I were hiding in the bathroom as she passed. I ran up to your room and Kemp left to follow Ruth to where she had left the car. You know, I felt at the time there was something strange about the way she tried to convince us that she had come by train and bus.'

Iris shivered. 'It's horrible to think someone wanted to kill me. Did she hate me, too?'

'Oh, I don't think so. But she didn't want her efforts to be for nothing. I'm sure Lucilla told her you had decided to marry me, which meant there was no time to lose. Once we were married, I would become the next <u>heir</u> to the fortune.'

'Poor Lucilla. I'm so sorry for her. Has Victor really been arrested?'

Race nodded. 'This morning, when he arrived in New York.'

'Was he going to marry Ruth?'

'She thought so. And I think she would have <u>got her way</u>.'

'Anthony, I don't like my money.'

'All right, sweetheart. I've got enough money of my own to keep a wife in comfort. Let's give yours away to charity.'

'I think I'll keep a little bit,' said Iris. 'So that if I ever wanted to, I could walk out and leave you.'

'I don't think that's the right attitude to begin married life with!' Anthony protested, laughing.

Colonel Race got up. 'I'm going to have tea with the Farradays.' He smiled broadly at Anthony. 'I don't suppose you're coming?'

Anthony shook his head and Race walked out of the room. He turned in the doorway and said, 'Good show,' before closing the door behind him.

'That,' said Anthony, 'is the highest mark of British approval.'

'He thought I had done it, didn't he?' asked Iris.

'It's not his fault. He has known so many beautiful spies, all stealing secret <u>formulas</u> and classified information, that he thinks it must always be the beautiful girl who did it!'

'So, how did you know I hadn't?'

'Oh, love, I suppose,' smiled Anthony Browne.

◆ Character list ◆

Rosemary Barton: the young wife of George Barton. She is dead at the beginning of the story.

Iris Marle: Rosemary's younger sister

Paul Bennett: Rosemary's very rich godfather. He is known as her 'uncle' – a close friend of Rosemary and Iris's mother, Viola Marle (now dead).

Hector Marle: the father (now dead) of Rosemary and Iris

George Barton: married to Rosemary. He is a wealthy businessman in the City of London.

Lucilla Drake: Iris and Rosemary's aunt (half-sister of Hector Marle), who lives with George and Iris

Stephen Farraday: a politician and member of the House of Commons in the British parliament

Anthony (Tony) Browne: a friend of Rosemary's, working in the armaments business

Vincent Drake: Lucilla Drake's son, and Rosemary's cousin

Lord Dewsbury: chairman of an armaments factory, and connected to Anthony Browne

Ruth Lessing: George's secretary

Lady Alexandra (Sandra) Farraday: Stephen Farraday's wife and the daughter of Lord and Lady Kidderminster. Her unmarried name was Alexandra Hayle.

Colonel Race: a friend of George Barton, who works with the British Intelligence service.

Lord and Lady Kidderminster: Sandra Farraday's parents. They are important in British politics. Their family surname is Hayle.

Charles: the head waiter at the Luxembourg restaurant

Giuseppe Bolsano: a waiter at the Luxembourg restaurant

Chief Inspector Kemp: a senior police offer at Scotland Yard, the main office of the London police

Gerald Tollington: an army officer, present at the Luxembourg restaurant

The Honorable Patricia Brice-Woodworth: present at the Luxembourg restaurant

Pedro Morales: a Mexican businessman

Christine Shannon: a friend of Pedro Morales

Betty Archdale: a former maid at Barton's house

Mary Rees-Talbot: Betty's next employer and friend of Colonel Race

Pierre: a junior waiter at the Luxembourg restaurant

Chloe West: a young actress

Sergeant Pollock: a police officer working for Chief Inspector Kemp

Monkey Coleman: an American criminal

◆ Cultural notes ◆

1. Cyanide poison

Agatha Christie worked as a pharmacist during the First and Second World Wars, and therefore had considerable knowledge of drugs and poisons. The cyanide which is referred to in the story is a white powder, similar in appearance to sugar, which dissolves easily in water or other liquids. It is very poisonous, and if a person swallows it, they are likely to die quickly. At the time Agatha Christie was writing, it was normal for people in the country to keep a form of cyanide in the garden shed to put on insect nests to kill them all quickly. Now it is against the law to possess such poisons.

2. Wills and inheritance

A will is a legal document that describes how the money and property left when someone dies is distributed to relatives and others. Many people from the upper classes (though by the 1950s this was changing significantly) did not have jobs, and lived from investments and inherited wealth. Women in particular were dependent on financial support from their husbands.

Property and land, on the death of the owner, would usually pass to the eldest son, but if a person did not have any children, such as Paul Bennett, he or she could choose who to leave their money to. In this story, Paul leaves all his money to Rosemary, but also makes special conditions about what should happen to his money if Rosemary also dies without having children. In this case it would go to her sister Iris.

3. Inquests

In cases of sudden, violent or suspicious death, it is common to hold a public inquiry called an inquest to find out why the person died. The coroner is the person in charge of the inquest, and the official cause of death is decided by a jury – a group of twelve ordinary people from the local area.

At the inquest the coroner and the jury hear medical evidence, as well as evidence from any other people that may be relevant. The family of the person who died, and members of the public can also attend the inquest.

Once all the evidence has been heard, the jury gives its verdict – for example, natural death, accidental death, suicide or murder.

4. Why Lucilla moved in with George and Iris
After Rosemary's death, it would be considered inappropriate for Iris to continue living with George Barton, because she is legally a child (being under 18) at the beginning of the story, and because George is now a single man. Therefore Aunt Lucilla is invited to join the household to ensure that Iris is protected. This keeps Iris's reputation safe – if there was any suspicion that she and George were living together as a couple, it would be difficult for both of them. At the time, it was common for young women to have an older woman to accompany them in social situations. Aunt Lucilla also accompanies Iris to parties and dances.

5. London's social world
It was customary for upper class and aristocratic families to participate in social events – usually dances – where their daughters could meet suitable men as prospective husbands, but in a controlled environment. The young women were called 'debutante', from the French word meaning 'beginning'. This process was called 'coming out' – i.e. the first time a young woman was presented to society. Aunt Lucilla takes on the role of helping Iris to 'come out' into society, and this is how she meets Anthony again.

6. Courting

This is the old-fashioned term for the period of time before a man and woman officially declare that they are engaged to be married. During this time, traditionally, the man would try to win the woman's affection by giving her gifts, taking her to nice places, and perhaps writing her letters and poetry or making other similar romantic gestures.

7. Country houses

Rich people often had large houses in the country as well as a house in London or another town, and lived comfortable lives with a lot of leisure time. They could choose to spend time in either house.

Weekends were busy times for such houses, as they would often have visitors and guests, who would participate in country activities like hunting and fishing. There would also be large meals and parties involving considerable expense and luxurious food and drink.

8. Conservative party

The Conservative party is the oldest political party in the UK and it is the party which the upper classes in Britain at the time of the story would usually have supported. The members of the Conservative party usually came from educated, upper class backgrounds, and protected the interests of their class. Their opponents, the Labour party, supported the views of the working classes.

Lord Kidderminster's comment that the Conservative party needs talented new members refers to the fact that the Labour party was gaining in popularity at the time (the story was published in 1945), and the Conservatives had to work hard to try to remain in power. In 1945, Labour won the general election and was in charge of Britain until 1951.

9. Houses of Parliament / House of Commons

The Houses of Parliament is the official building where the government of the United Kingdom meets and works. The House of Commons is the name for the group of MPs who are elected by people to represent their views.

10. Mayfair

This is an area of central London, and at the time of the story, it was home to many people from the upper classes, like the Kidderminsters. It was – and still is – an area where the inhabitants had a lot of money and lived comfortable lives. The area of Mayfair is bordered by Hyde Park (the park where Stephen and Sandra walked together), Piccadilly, Bond Street and Oxford Street.

11. MP

MP stands for Member of Parliament. Britain is divided into different areas called constituencies, and each constituency elects an MP to represent their views in the Houses of Parliament. In the story, Stephen Farraday has been elected by the people to have a seat in the House of Commons. At the time of the story in England, only men and women over the age of twenty-one could vote for who they wanted to elect as their MP. Now the voting age is eighteen.

12. The Borgias

This is a reference to an important Italian family who were powerful in the late 1400s and early 1500s. They are famous for committing many crimes, including murder, theft and bribery. They were known for using poison to kill their enemies.

13. Being of age / under age

In 1753 a law was made in Britain which said that a person under the age of 21 could not get married without the permission of their parents or legal guardians. Therefore Iris is unable to marry Anthony unless

Lucilla and George Barton agree. Anthony is hoping to make special arrangements to perform a marriage even though Iris is under age, by applying to a priest who he knows. For this, he would need a special licence which makes the marriage legal even though it does not follow the usual laws.

14. Servants

In England at this time, the richer members of society – the upper classes – employed servants to do many things. A cook would prepare all the meals, and a parlourmaid would serve the meals in the dining room. There could also be people to do the gardening and take care of the house. The ladies of the family sometimes had personal servants who looked after their clothes. In smaller houses there might be one or two servants who did all the work between them. By the end of World War II, though, this situation was starting to change and people had fewer servants.

15. Scotland Yard

Scotland Yard is the headquarters of the British police – it is situated near the Houses of Parliament in central London. In the story, Colonel Kemp, an old friend of Race's, is based there.

16. Making social visits

A social visit is a term for a visit from a friend which is just made for social, personal reasons. Mrs Rees-Talbot is surprised to see Colonel Race because he is usually busy, and he doesn't visit friends just for social reasons.

17. The ghost of Banquo

In the William Shakespeare play *Macbeth*, Banquo is a character who starts as a friend of the leading character Macbeth. As Macbeth wants to become more powerful, he has Banquo murdered, but his ghost returns during a big celebration, and this terrifies Macbeth.

◆ Glossary ◆

absent-minded ADJECTIVE
Someone who is **absent-minded** forgets things or does not pay attention to what they are doing, often because they are thinking about something else.

acrobat COUNTABLE NOUN
An **acrobat** is an entertainer who performs difficult physical acts such as jumping and balancing.

admirer COUNTABLE NOUN
A woman's **admirers** are men who are attracted to her.

adore TRANSITIVE VERB
If you **adore** someone, you feel great love and admiration for them.

advisor COUNTABLE NOUN
An **advisor** is someone whose job is to give someone help and advice about what they should do.

affectionately ADVERB
If you do something **affectionately**, you do it in a way that shows you like or love someone.

All Souls' Day UNCOUNTABLE NOUN
All Souls' Day is the 2nd of November, a Christian festival when prayers are said for the souls of the dead.

anonymous ADJECTIVE
An **anonymous** letter does not include the name of the person who wrote it.

armaments PLURAL NOUN
Armaments are weapons and military equipment belonging to an army or country.

aspirin COUNTABLE NOUN
An **aspirin** is a pill containing a mild drug which reduces pain and fever.

attendant COUNTABLE NOUN
An **attendant** is someone whose job is to serve or help people in a place such as a public toilet or cloakroom.

attic COUNTABLE NOUN
An **attic** is a room at the top of a house just below the roof.

befriend TRANSITIVE VERB
If you **befriend** someone, especially someone who is lonely, you make friends with them.

beggar COUNTABLE NOUN
A **beggar** is someone who lives by asking people for money or food.

beloved ADJECTIVE
A **beloved** person is one that you feel great love for.

betray TRANSITIVE VERB
If you **betray** someone, you hurt them by doing something bad to them when they trusted you. If you **betray** someone's secrets, you reveal their secrets when they trusted you not to.

binoculars PLURAL NOUN
Binoculars consist of two small telescopes joined together side by side, which you look through in order to see things that are a long way away.

bitterly ADVERB
If you cry **bitterly**, you cry a lot with strong, unpleasant emotions such as anger or dislike.

blackmail UNCOUNTABLE NOUN
Blackmail is the action of threatening to reveal a secret about someone, unless they do something you tell them to do, such as giving you money.

bloodshot ADJECTIVE
If your eyes are **bloodshot**, the parts that are usually white are red or pink.

blotting paper UNCOUNTABLE NOUN
Blotting paper is thick soft paper that you use for soaking up and drying ink on a piece of paper.

boarding school COUNTABLE NOUN
A **boarding school** is a school which some or all of the pupils live in during the school term.

briefcase COUNTABLE NOUN
A **briefcase** is a case used for carrying documents in.

butler COUNTABLE NOUN
A **butler** is the most important male servant in a wealthy house.

cabaret COUNTABLE NOUN
A **cabaret** is a show that is performed in a restaurant or nightclub, and that consists of dancing, singing, or comedy acts.

calculating ADJECTIVE
If you describe someone as **calculating**, you disapprove of the fact that they deliberately plan to get what they want, often by hurting or harming other people.

canon COUNTABLE NOUN
A **canon** is a member of the clergy who is on the staff of a cathedral.

chap COUNTABLE NOUN
A **chap** is a man or boy.

choke INTRANSITIVE VERB
When you **choke**, you cannot breathe properly or get enough air into your lungs.

classified ADJECTIVE
Classified information or documents are officially secret.

Colonel COUNTABLE NOUN
A **colonel** is a senior officer in an army, air force, or the marines.

come to trial PHRASE
If a case **comes to trial**, it is heard in a law court by a judge and jury, who listen to evidence and decide whether someone is guilty of a crime.

compact COUNTABLE NOUN
A **compact** is a small, flat case that contains face powder and a mirror.

conjuring trick COUNTABLE NOUN
A **conjuring trick** is a trick in which something is made to appear or disappear as if by magic.

consent UNCOUNTABLE NOUN
Consent is permission to do something.

convict TRANSITIVE VERB
If someone is **convicted** of a crime, they are found guilty of that crime in a law court.

cyanide UNCOUNTABLE NOUN
Cyanide is a very strong poison which can kill people.

dearest ADJECTIVE
You can call someone **dearest** when you are very fond of them.

destined ADJECTIVE
If someone is **destined** for something, that thing seems certain to happen to them or be done by them.

devotion UNCOUNTABLE NOUN
Devotion is great love, affection, or admiration for someone.

directory COUNTABLE NOUN
A **directory** is a book which gives lists of facts, for example people's names, addresses, and telephone numbers, usually arranged in alphabetical order.

dismay UNCOUNTABLE NOUN
Dismay is a strong feeling of fear, worry, or shock that is caused by something unpleasant and unexpected.

disposition COUNTABLE NOUN
Someone's **disposition** is the way that they tend to behave or feel.

dock COUNTABLE NOUN
A **dock** is an enclosed area in a harbour where ships go to be loaded, unloaded, and repaired.

doorway COUNTABLE NOUN
A **doorway** is a space in a wall where a door opens and closes.

drive COUNTABLE NOUN
A **drive** is a wide piece of hard ground, or sometimes a private road, that leads from the road to a person's house.

emerald COUNTABLE NOUN
An **emerald** is a precious stone which is clear and bright green.

enchanting ADJECTIVE
If you describe someone or something as **enchanting**, you mean that they are very attractive or charming.

escort TRANSITIVE VERB
If you **escort** someone somewhere, you accompany them there.

exclaim TRANSITIVE VERB
If someone **exclaims** something, they say it suddenly, loudly, or emphatically, often because they are excited, shocked, or angry.

fancy dress UNCOUNTABLE NOUN
Fancy dress is clothing that you wear, for example at a party, that makes you look like a famous person or a person from a story, from history, or from a particular profession.

farewell party COUNTABLE NOUN
A **farewell party** is a party held in order to say goodbye to someone who is leaving a place or going on a journey.

fellow COUNTABLE NOUN
A **fellow** is an old-fashioned word for a man or boy.

feverish ADJECTIVE
Feverish emotion is characterized by extreme nervousness or excitement.

fingerprint COUNTABLE NOUN
Fingerprints are marks made by a person's fingers which show the lines on the skin. Everyone's fingerprints are different, so they can be used to identify criminals.

finish off PHRASAL VERB
If someone **finishes** a person **off**, they kill them.

fitting ADJECTIVE
Something that is **fitting** is right or suitable.

flirtation VARIABLE NOUN
Flirtation is the act of behaving as if you are sexually attracted to someone, in a playful or not very serious way.

footstep COUNTABLE NOUN
A **footstep** is the sound that is made by someone walking when their foot touches the ground.

for her sake PHRASE
When you do something **for** someone's **sake**, you do it in order to help them or make them happy.

forge TRANSITIVE VERB
If someone **forges** something such as a banknote or a document, they make a copy of it that looks genuine, in order to deceive people.

formula COUNTABLE NOUN
The **formula** for a substance is a list of the amounts of various ingredients which make it up.

fortune-hunter COUNTABLE NOUN
If you say that someone is a **fortune-hunter**, you mean that they are trying to marry or have a relationship with someone rich because they want to get their money.

frown INTRANSITIVE VERB
When someone **frowns**, their eyebrows become drawn together, because they are annoyed, worried, or puzzled, or because they are thinking.

gesture COUNTABLE NOUN
A **gesture** is something that you say or do in order to create a certain effect.

get your way PHRASE
If someone **gets their way**, they do what they want to do, or things happen in the way that they want.

gloomy ADJECTIVE
A **gloomy** day is cloudy and dark.

goddaughter, godfather, godmother COUNTABLE NOUN
A young person's **godfather** or **godmother** is a man or woman who their parents have chosen to have a special relationship with them, and to help bring them up

in the Christian religion. You can say that the young person is this person's **goddaughter** or **godson**.

goodness me PHRASE
People sometimes say '**goodness me**' to express surprise.

grieving ADJECTIVE
Someone who is **grieving** is feeling very sad, usually because someone they love has recently died.

hangman's rope PHRASE
The **hangman's rope** is sometimes used to refer to death by hanging, usually as punishment for a crime.

headmaster COUNTABLE NOUN
A **headmaster** is a man who is the head teacher of a school.

heir COUNTABLE NOUN
An **heir** is someone who has the right to inherit a person's money, property, or title when that person dies.

hollow COUNTABLE NOUN
A **hollow** is an area that is lower than the surrounding surface.

horrid ADJECTIVE
If you describe someone or something as **horrid**, you mean that they are very unpleasant.

housekeeping UNCOUNTABLE NOUN
Housekeeping is the work and organization involved in running a home, including the shopping and cleaning.

hymn COUNTABLE NOUN
A **hymn** is a religious song that Christians sing in church.

hysterics PLURAL NOUN
If someone is in **hysterics**, they are in a state of uncontrolled shock, anger, or panic.

in trust PHRASE
If money or property that someone owns is **in trust**, it is kept and invested for them.

incriminating ADJECTIVE
Incriminating evidence suggests that someone is responsible for something bad, especially a crime.

indignantly ADVERB
If you say something **indignantly**, you say it in a shocked and angry way, because you think that something is unjust or unfair.

influenza UNCOUNTABLE NOUN
Influenza, or **flu**, is an illness which is similar to a bad cold but more serious. It often makes you feel very weak and makes your muscles hurt.

inherit TRANSITIVE VERB
If you **inherit** money or property, you receive it from someone who has died.

inquest COUNTABLE NOUN
When an **inquest** is held, a public official hears evidence about someone's death in order to find out the cause.

-like SUFFIX
-like is used after a noun to make an adjective that describes something as similar to or typical of the noun. For example 'business-like' means 'in an efficient or unemotional way, as you would do in business'.

lipstick COUNTABLE NOUN
A **lipstick** is a small tube containing a coloured substance which women put on their lips.

lord COUNTABLE NOUN
In Britain, a **lord** is a man who has a high rank in the nobility. **Lord** is used in the title of a man of this rank, for example 'Lord Sainsbury'.

loser COUNTABLE NOUN
If you refer to someone as a **loser**, you have a low opinion of them because you think they are always unsuccessful.

lust UNCOUNTABLE NOUN
Lust is a feeling of strong sexual desire for someone.

maid COUNTABLE NOUN
A **maid** is a woman who works as a servant in a hotel or private house.

mat COUNTABLE NOUN
A **mat** is a small piece of carpet or other thick material which is put on the floor for protection, decoration, or comfort.

mission COUNTABLE NOUN
A **mission** is an important task that people are given to do, especially one that involves travelling to another country.

mistress COUNTABLE NOUN
A married man's **mistress** is a woman who is not his wife and with whom he is having a sexual relationship.

mocking ADJECTIVE
If you say something in a **mocking** way, you show or pretend that you think someone is foolish, for example by saying something funny about them, or by imitating their behaviour.

Morello cherry COUNTABLE NOUN
A **Morello cherry** is a dark kind of cherry with a sour taste, used in cooking.

nest COUNTABLE NOUN
A **nest** is a home that a group of insects or other creatures make in order to live in and give birth to their young in.

nudge TRANSITIVE VERB
If you **nudge** someone, you push them gently, usually with your elbow, in order to draw their attention to something.

observant ADJECTIVE
Someone who is **observant** pays a lot of attention to things and notices more about them than most people do.

on a golden plate PHRASE
If you say that someone has things handed to them **on a golden plate**, you disapprove of them because they have got a lot of good things without having to work or try hard.

overdo TRANSITIVE VERB
If someone **overdoes** something, they behave in an exaggerated or extreme way.

overdose COUNTABLE NOUN
If someone takes an **overdose** of a drug, they take more of it than is safe.

oyster COUNTABLE NOUN
An **oyster** is a large flat shellfish that is often eaten raw.

parliamentary ADJECTIVE
Parliamentary is used to describe things that are connected with a parliament or with Members of Parliament.

parlour COUNTABLE NOUN
A **parlour** is a room in a house for sitting in.

parlourmaid COUNTABLE NOUN
In former times, a **parlourmaid** was a female servant in a private house whose job involved serving people at table.

penal servitude UNCOUNTABLE NOUN
Penal servitude is the punishment of being kept in prison and forced to do hard physical work.

pole COUNTABLE NOUN
A **pole** is a long thin piece of wood or metal, used especially for supporting things.

porter COUNTABLE NOUN
A **porter** is a person whose job is to carry things, for example people's luggage at a railway station or in a hotel.

promising ADJECTIVE
Someone or something that is **promising** seems likely to be very good or successful.

prosecute TRANSITIVE VERB
If the authorities **prosecute** someone, they charge them with a crime and put them on trial.

psychiatrist COUNTABLE NOUN
A **psychiatrist** is a doctor who treats people suffering from mental illness.

reassure TRANSITIVE VERB
If you **reassure** someone, you say or do things to make them stop worrying about something.

reluctantly ADVERB
If you do something **reluctantly**, you do it after hesitating because you do not really want to do it or are not sure about it.

resent TRANSITIVE VERB
If you **resent** something, you feel bitter and angry about it.

robe COUNTABLE NOUN
A **robe** is a long, loose piece of clothing which covers all of your body. People sometimes wear a robe when they are relaxing at home or have just had a bath or shower.

rustle INTRANSITIVE VERB
A **rustle** is a soft dry sound made by something moving, for example in a tree or bush.

sabotage TRANSITIVE VERB
If a machine, railway line, or bridge is **sabotaged**, it is deliberately damaged or destroyed, for example by an enemy in a war.

sachet COUNTABLE NOUN
A **sachet** is a small closed paper or plastic bag, containing a small quantity of something.

sacrifice TRANSITIVE VERB
If you **sacrifice** something that is valuable or important, you give it up, usually to obtain something else for yourself or for other people.

seal TRANSITIVE VERB
If you **seal** an opening, you cover it with something in order to prevent air, liquid, or other material getting in or out.

seat COUNTABLE NOUN
If someone has a **seat** in a parliament, congress, or senate, they have been elected as a member of it.

sensual ADJECTIVE
Someone who is **sensual** shows a great liking for physical pleasures, especially sexual pleasures.

settle down PHRASAL VERB
When someone **settles down**, they start living a quiet life in one place, especially when they get married or buy a house.

shrug TRANSITIVE VERB
If you **shrug** your shoulders, you raise them to show that you are not interested in something or that you do not know or care about something.

slash TRANSITIVE VERB
To **slash** something means to make a long, deep cut in it.

snap TRANSITIVE VERB
If you **snap** something, you say it in a sharp, unfriendly way.

sober ADJECTIVE
A **sober** person has not drunk or does not drink too much alcohol.

soda UNCOUNTABLE NOUN
Soda is fizzy water used for mixing with alcoholic drinks and fruit juice.

sparkle INTRANSITIVE VERB
If your eyes **sparkle**, they are bright and shining, especially because you are happy or excited.

spell COUNTABLE NOUN
If you say that a **spell** is broken, you mean that a situation in which someone seemed to be controlled or very fascinated by something or by another person suddenly ends.

splendid ADJECTIVE
If you say that something is **splendid**, you mean that it is very good.

stick together PHRASAL VERB
If people **stick together**, they stay with each other and support each other.

stir up PHRASAL VERB
If you **stir up** trouble or stir things up, you cause trouble.

stun TRANSITIVE VERB
If you are **stunned** by something, you are extremely shocked or surprised by it and are therefore unable to speak or do anything.

subconsciously ADVERB
If you feel something **subconsciously**, that feeling can influence you or affect your behaviour even though you are not aware of it.

summon TRANSITIVE VERB
If you **summon** someone, you order them to come to you.

suspect COUNTABLE NOUN
A **suspect** is a person who the police or authorities think may be guilty of a crime.

sweetheart COUNTABLE NOUN
You call someone **sweetheart** if you are very fond of them.

tactic COUNTABLE NOUN
Tactics are the methods that you choose to use in order to achieve what you want in a particular situation.

tamper with PHRASAL VERB
If someone ta**mpers with** something such as evidence, they interfere with it or try to change it when they have no right to do so.

tangle up PHRASAL VERB
If something is **tangled up** in something such as wire or ropes, they are caught or trapped in it.

tank COUNTABLE NOUN
A **tank** is a large military vehicle that is equipped with weapons and moves along on metal tracks that are fitted over the wheels.

tear-stained ADJECTIVE
If someone's face is **tear-stained**, you can see that they have been crying.

telegram COUNTABLE NOUN
A **telegram** was a message that was sent by telegraph and then printed and delivered to someone's home or office.

thank goodness PHRASE
You can say '**Thank goodness**' when you are very relieved about something.

toast COUNTABLE NOUN
When you drink a **toast** to someone or something, you lift a glass, usually containing an alcoholic drink, and drink from it as a symbolic gesture, in order to show your appreciation of them or to wish them success.

trap COUNTABLE NOUN
A **trap** is a trick that is intended to catch or deceive someone.

try (his) hand PHRASE
If you **try your hand** at an activity, you attempt to do it, usually for the first time.

twisted ADJECTIVE
If something is **twisted**, it has moved or been moved into an unusual, uncomfortable, or bent position.

undercover ADVERB
If someone is working **undercover**, they are working to secretly obtain information for the government or the police.

undercurrent COUNTABLE NOUN
If there is an **undercurrent** of a feeling, it influences the way you think or behave although you may not be aware of it.

unfold TRANSITIVE VERB
If someone **unfolds** something such as a piece of paper, they open it out and make it flat after it has been folded.

velvet UNCOUNTABLE NOUN
Velvet is soft material made from cotton, silk, or nylon, which has a thick layer of smooth short threads on one side.

verdict COUNTABLE NOUN
In a court of law, the **verdict** is the decision that is given by the jury or judge at the end of a trial.

villain COUNTABLE NOUN
A **villain** is someone who deliberately harms other people or breaks the law in order to get what he or she wants.

weep INTRANSITIVE VERB
If someone **weeps**, they cry.

wicked ADJECTIVE
you use **wicked** to describe someone who is very bad.

will COUNTABLE NOUN
A **will** is a document in which you declare what you want to happen to your money and property when you die.

worship TRANSITIVE VERB
If you **worship** someone or something, you love them or admire them very much.

COLLINS ENGLISH READERS

Do you want to read more at your reading level?
Try these:

AGATHA CHRISTIE MYSTERIES

Crooked House 978-0-00-826235-8
They Do It With Mirrors 978-0-00-826236-5
A Pocket Full of Rye 978-0-00-826237-2
Destination Unknown 978-0-00-826238-9
4.50 From Paddington 978-0-00-826239-6
Cat Among the Pigeons 978-0-00-826240-2
Appointment with Death 978-0-00-826233-4
Peril at End House 978-0-00-826232-7
The Murder at the Vicarage 978-0-00-826231-0

Find out more at **www.collinselt.com/readers**